Believe

Chasing Shadows Book One

by
Mia Fox

Believed, Chasing Shadows Book One by Mia Fox
Published by Evatopia Press
http://www.evatopia.com
8447 Wilshire Blvd., Ste. 401, Beverly Hills, CA 90211
a division of Evatopia, Inc.

ISBN: 978-1-63099-014-5

Formatting by Bob Houston eBook Formatting
Bob_Houston@hotmail.com

Stay in touch with Mia Fox
Twitter @MiaFoxBooks
Facebook www.facebook.com/MiaFoxBooks

Dedication

For my family --

I love you from here to there...the long way
around.
Thank you for 'believing' in me always.

Forward

One never knows when inspiration will strike. Fortunately for writers, it happens often and in frequently unexplainable circumstances. The inspiration for this book was inspired by the beautiful words of Aimee Mann in her song, "Save Me."

You look like...a perfect fit,
For a girl in need...of a tourniquet.
But can you save me?
Come on and save me...

Chapter 1 - Ella

Dear Nate,

I've been counting down the days until your return for so long that I can hardly believe the end is near. One more week! Those are nearly the three sweetest words that exist...right after I love you!

I've got a list of things we're going to do when you return. Get ready for all of your favorites: hiking (our special place), picnic (with pastries from La Conversation, of course!), and I've been shopping...I'll include a photo of me in my new lingerie.

So soldier, you better be in top-notch shape. I can't wait to see you.

Love,
Ella

Chapter 2 - Nate

I held the letter close. It smelled like her perfume, which coupled with the photo of her in a barely there nightie, had my heart racing for reasons beyond the continual explosions that occurred at a proximity that was certainly closer than comfort level.

You never really get used to always being on alert, away from loved ones, missing the comfort of home. And yet, some of these men are adrenaline junkies, signing up for tour after tour. I was falling into that trap, but this is my last one. I've had enough and if I were a cat, I'd say I'm getting close to using up my nine lives.

Another blast occurred, this one closer than we were expecting and our Sergeant Major ordered us to run for another barricade. In the shuffle, the letter and its corresponding photo slipped from my fingers. It was just pieces of paper, but it was all I had at night to keep me from going crazy and I read those letters from Ella over and over again. I ran back in the midst of dirt raining down, clouds of dust and the continual sounds of explosions.

Through it all, I could hear the Sergeant's voice, both angry as hell and worried. But I made it back.

"You are one lucky idiot," he noted when I returned to the barricade still clutching the photo. His neck craned toward me so he could sneak a glance at what I was willing to die for. "She must be some girl."

Chapter 3 - Ella

I folded up the nightie that I had just posed coquettishly in. Nate had inadvertently helped pick it out before he left, mentioning that it was his favorite from the Victoria's Secret catalog. The mailing seemed to arrive on a weekly basis, proving that I order way too much. But he's worth it.

I remember the game we played the night before he left when he admired it. We were lying on my bed, thumbing through the pages of the catalog...

He was kissing my neck, layering his words as well as his mouth over me, playfully kissing my toes and working his way upward. "Ella, if anything ever happened to me..." his mouth idled when he reached my waist.

"Mmmm? Nothing's going to happen to you because I need this too much."

He kept kissing me, now moving his mouth upwards, teasing each breast and then along my neck, finally meeting my own lips and pressing against me ever so gently to push me back against the bed. "But if it did...I'd want you to..." he stopped talking as I pressed myself against him.

"You'd want me to do this?" I teased.

"Seriously Ella, I'd want you to go on with your life. Live it to the fullest and find someone."

I propped myself up on my elbows suddenly. "Wow Nate, talk about a mood killer."

"I'm sorry. It's just...something that I think about."

"Well don't," I told him, but Nate was relentless, as if he needed to be sure that I would be okay if he wasn't around. "What about you? What if I'm the one to go first?"

"If we were in Vegas they'd put odds on me going first."

I grabbed the Victoria's Secret catalog once again. "You never know. This could end up being the next Mrs. Nate Holden," I said pointing to a picture of a brunette beauty with ice blue eyes.

He admired the photo. "In that case...you never told me I'd be marrying Adriana Lima."

"Oh my god, you know her name!" I said and playfully swatted his butt with the rolled up catalog.

"She's a Victoria's Secret model. Every guy knows her name. But, there's no other woman for me," he said and pulled me back into his arms.

I nuzzled his neck. "Me too."

"No other woman for you?"

"No other man, smart ass."

"You would find someone. You're too insatiable," he said enjoying the kisses that I layered down his chest to his stomach. But his words bothered me. I had to stop just as I was about to reach the good bit.

"What do you mean? I love you."

"But you would go on...I need to know that."

I pressed a finger to his lips and shushed him. "Don't," I said shaking my head. "I can't think about that."

"Ella, life is for living."

"It's our last night...let's not waste it arguing. In fact..." I said with a glimmer in my eye and a mischievous tone to my voice, "we don't need to talk at all."

I pushed Nate onto his back and climbed on top of him. Immediately I felt him harden underneath me as I kissed him. He had both arms around my waist, holding me close and making me feel safe in his grip. With one quick movement, he flipped me over. I slid my hands over his back, feeling the taunt muscles and moving downward to where his waist narrowed. His shirt was off, but I furrowed my brow in frustration when my hands reached the waistband of his sweats.

"Off," was all I had to say.

He grabbed at my own shorts and with a tug had them down to my ankles for me to shimmy out of.

"I meant yours!"

Nate smiled at me. "I know, but I couldn't resist. Get this off too," he said pulling at my top.

Within seconds we were skin to skin, and once again mouth to mouth.

"I love you, Ella," he murmured against me.

"Come home soon."

"You know I will."

His knee pressed lightly against my inner thigh, coaxing me to do what I already wanted.

Chapter 4 - Nate

The main objectives of Operation Dragon Strike had been accomplished and yet we were still in the Kandahar province of Afghanistan, holding up a presence in case another counter-insurgent mission was called upon. The Taliban forces had been pushed back, but this was considered the birthplace of their movement and until all air strikes in the region had ceased, we were told to make ourselves at home.

The operation's mission was to reclaim the strategic southern province. Led by my unit, the 101st Airborne Division, also known as FAST, Fleet Anti-terrorism Security Team, we were tasked with ensuring that this major supply route into the city was clear and safe for passage. But first, we would have to get through the Zhari District, where some of the heaviest fighting I had seen since my tour started was taking place.

The day was quiet as we started toward our next target, the Arghandab District, but that all changed. A small boy was seen walking toward our platoon. He was crying and walking alone. I could hear his cries, but I struggled to make out the source of his anguish. Initially, I assumed he was just another civilian casualty, a boy who had lost his family. Our operation was drawing criticism from the locals because of supposed heavy-handed tactics by the U.S. military that had destroyed civilian homes and farms.

"What's this?" one of the thirty-five men asked, indicating the boy.

I shook my head, still struggling to see what was different about the boy. He looked as if he was struggling to walk properly.

"He's loaded! Strapped with an IED!" one of the corporals shouted, and sure enough that's when we all noticed it. A large bomb pack, in this case an improvised explosive device, was attached to his mid-section, which was no doubt the reason he moved so gingerly.

"Get your men outta here," the Major barked, but I was already on it.

"Cover! Take cover!" I yelled.

Some of the men started to scream at the boy to go back, as they ran in the opposite direction. I was the only one who approached him, slowly and calmly.

"Second Lieutenant Holden you are ordered to retreat."

I stopped in my tracks, positioned between the boy crying in front of me and my Major behind me. "I can do it," I called back, not quite sure who I was sending the message to.

"You have permission, but you're not taking anyone with you. You call it out, and I'll talk it through with you."

I nodded my assent to my superior, and continued toward the boy, holding my hands out to him, showing him I meant him no harm. In actuality, he didn't seem at all scared of me. As I got right in front of him, he whimpered and spoke in perfect English. "Mister, I'm going to die today."

"No you're not. Don't think like that. I'm going to help you," I said with more confidence than I felt. I examined the crisscrossing wires that lined the bomb pack and closed my eyes in a quick prayer.

"You can do it?"

His worried words brought me back.

I swallowed and removed a pair of wire cutters from my own pack. I fingered the wires -- red, blue, green, white, and black. Two were dummies. Two were triggers. The other was a wild card, designed to go off if the first two were cut in the wrong order.

"What've you got?" my commanding officer yelled.

The sun was high in the sky and beads of sweat dotted my forehead as I contemplated the framework of the bomb. All the while it maintained a steady and infuriating ticking. "I've got the back removed. Definitely homemade. It'll explode ball bearings, maybe bolts too. The shock waves will travel outward at about 1,600 feet per second."

Upon hearing that last bit, he ordered the rest of the men to retreat even further. They didn't have to be told twice.

"Continue," he ordered once everyone else was in the safety zone.

I traced the wires to the opening at the back of the bomb, took a deep breath and cut the blue wire, which was first in line. So far so good. The black one was next, but intertwined twice, once around the red and once around the white, making it harder to get to, which made me believe it was the right one to focus on. With another careful clip, the ticking stopped and the boy threw his arms around my neck.

Relief flooded through me and I gave the thumbs up sign, only to have a bomb dropped from above, landing just a few feet away. Instinctually, I kept my arms around the boy and felt myself lifted off the ground and thrown. Dirt rained down around us and the shouts of our men echoed in my ears. Screaming. Running. And then, blackness.

Chapter 5 - Ella

I stared at the coffin, noticing the spray of white gerber daisies and white roses that draped over its top.

"He would have liked the simplicity of it," I said and squeezed Nate's hand.

"Yeah, he was a good guy. Thanks for being here."

"Are you kidding? Where else would I be?"

Nate had been given a month long furlough home for "rest and recovery." The dangerous nature of his job meant that he was always given twelve weeks home and then another six to ten weeks on the job, but he was sent home early this time after having lost a fellow "devil dog" as they called each other. Nate told me about the bomb, the ensuing attack that was in place in case their first attempt didn't work, and the fellow Marine who was also from Los Angeles, but would never make it home.

The other funeral attendees had started to return to their cars, but I sensed that

Nate needed a minute more by the graveside.

"I'll wait for you in the car."

"I'll just be a minute."

I nodded and gave him a kiss on the cheek. It felt smooth under my lips and he smelled of a clean, outdoorsy scent that I never forgot even when he was away. This was a horrible reason for him to be sent home, but I couldn't help think that I was lucky to have him for a few extra weeks. I was damned sure that I would make the most of it.

# # #

Just a few days later, we put the tragedy that sent Nate home behind us and resumed our vow to create happier times.

"Want a bite?" I pinched off a piece of my almond croissant and popped it in my mouth. It was still warm from the oven, its smell so enticing that I could never resist trying it right out of the bakery's pink box. The idea that I was supposed to wait until we were on the trail was baffling to me. We drove along Mulholland Highway near Calabasas until Nate and I reached the hidden marker off Stunt Road, a tiny offshoot from the highway. It was our favorite Sunday hike, hidden from the rest of the world due to its remote access and lack of signage. Other than the bakery stop, this was my favorite routine of ours, one that started before he left for Afghanistan and would continue every time he got back again.

"I have will power," he teased.

I turned and took in the sight of his hand on the wheel, the muscles in his arm bulging and then I couldn't resist but run a finger along his bicep. "Yes, you're terribly strong...but hungry."

"Alright, pop me off a piece," he said opening his mouth.

I held it in front of him and he took it, keeping his eye on the curve of the road, his smile showing his approval.

"It's too good not to eat while it's hot."

"We go through this every weekend," he said laughing. "You're like a little kid. Do I have to tell you that we'll be there in five minutes?"

"Alright, I'm putting it away," I said placing the rest back in the box, but not before stealing one last crumb. "You rest in here with Mr. Chocolate Croissant. Mommy will be right back to gobble you up."

"This is why I need to make an honest woman of you and get down on one knee. Oh wait...I already did that," he said smiling.

I gave him an embarrassed eye roll as he continued.

"Then, we'll have loads of babies and you won't have to talk to the pasties anymore."

"Mmm, that sounds...nice."

Nate leaned over to kiss me on the cheek and then took my hand and lightly caressed the top with his thumb. "One day..."

His words echoed in my mind. One day...but in just a month, Nate would leave for Afghanistan again. Even though his time away was short compared to most soldiers, I knew it was because the likelihood of something happening to him was higher than most. All he could tell me about his job was that he did reconnaissance missions -- being the first to go into an area to clear it for other platoons. Nate was good at his job, one of the best, in fact. But still, I worried that one day his luck would wear out. "You've got that look on your face," he noted. "Ella?"

"I'm fine."

"Oh, now that was convincing."

I knew I should snap out of it. Live for the day, enjoy the moment and all that rhetoric. But it was so hard to not think about the future. After all, isn't that what Nate was doing when he asked me to marry him? And now, he was waiting for my answer. It had been two days since he asked me, and I don't know why I was holding back. I loved him with all my heart, but the idea of him thinking too much about me and our future while being in a dangerous situation worried me. I wanted him to focus on himself when he was in the field. He didn't need extra responsibilities back home weighing on his mind.

Nate brought my hand up to his lips and lightly slid my knuckles back and forth over his mouth. For a guy he had the softest lips. We turned off the highway and pulled the car onto the shoulder where the marker for our weekly hike was practically hidden, but he didn't drop my hand. Instead, he pulled me closer to him and kissed me on the mouth.

"You taste like chocolate! You sneak! You're going to pay for that."

"The almond croissant was lonely in my stomach," I said by way of explanation, my mood brightening with his teasing.

"I'm going to call in all of my favors."

"Oh yeah?" My interest was definitely peaking.

"Yeah," he said and leaned in to kiss me again. This time it was longer, slower, and with intention.

When we stepped from the car, I raised my eyebrows and decided to grab the picnic blanket from the backseat. I wrapped it around my shoulders before reaching for my coveted pink bakery box, and headed toward the nearly hidden trail head. "Maybe our hike will have to wait," I teased.

Nate grabbed the cup holder with my mocha and his chai tea latte, then caught up to me and pulled my hand into his pocket. We walked like that for a few feet, my hand in his, feeling content and happy that we had the day to ourselves.

"Meadow in the woods?" he asked.

It was our spot. Our hidden hideaway where nobody ever hiked except for us. We had nearly worked our way through the guidebook of hikes through the Santa Monica Mountains National Recreation Area when we came to the Red Rock Canyon Trail. None compared to this one in my mind for the simple reason that it was so secluded. And, where exercise was concerned, this hike kicked my butt.

It was steep in spots, but in spite of that, Nate and I would run it. Slowing only when it was beyond possible to run and even then we scrambled on all fours, grabbing hold of roots to pull ourselves upwards as fast as our muscles would allow. Trail running with rocks and pebbles threatening to turn over our ankles, poisoned oak that stretched into the path and threatened to brush us as we passed, along with the occasional rattler that sunned itself on the trail were all part of the activity. I had adopted Nate's soldier mentality and half the fun of the rigorous work out was avoiding the perils.

I still wasn't in as good of shape as Nate, but I could hold my own. Except there were some days when the pressures of his job weighed on his mind and he needed to do an extra round. Then, I would do my best to keep up, thinking that I had made it to the end, only to learn that he had other ideas in mind like running back to the car. It was amazing how he moved like a deer, never wiping out in spite of the loose dirt and slippery terrain. But today, I wasn't going to entertain that activity. I was going to wipe away at least some of the uncertainty that our lives held. I may not be able to watch over Nate when he was on a mission, but I could give him what he wanted here at home.

I looked up at his smiling eyes, blue as the sky with the slightest tinge of green around the edges. What the hell was wrong with me? Why couldn't I just say that little word? Yes, yes, yes. My mind was shouting it at me. But I held back. Maybe because it scared me to death that he would be worrying about me at home rather than taking care of himself in the field. I brushed the thoughts away and focused on the present.

"We don't want our coffee or pastries to go cold. That would be a shame."

"Ahh, but I came prepared," he said holding up an air tight cooler.

I could see I was going to have to pull out the big guns. I sidled up to him, wrapped my arms around his waist and leaned in to whisper in his ear, "I've got a blanket and I know just what to do with it."

"So, I take it we're not going trail running today? We're having a picnic?"

I smiled a mischievous grin and laid out the blanket in the middle of our meadow. "That's not exactly what I had in mind." I sat down and patted the ground next to me. Nate smiled down at me.

"What do you have planned for me, little minx?"

"It's a secret. Come closer and I'll whisper it."

He plopped himself down and I leaned forward and lightly nibbled his ear lobe.

"Sorry? Were you saying something? I can't quite make it out, but I think you were trying to tell me..." and then, without a moment's hesitation, he wrapped his muscled arms around my waist and leaned into me, pressing his body on top of mine. We were right there in the midst of this gorgeous meadow, open for anyone to see, but nobody would. We were alone. The sun was shining through the trees and when Nate kissed me and ran his hand along my waist and upwards, I didn't have a care, not even one.

I looked up at him and took in his smile, his auburn hair catching the rays of sunlight and looking like spun honey. I reached up to brush his cheek, but he caught my hand in his own and gently brought it to his lips.

"Right here," I said tapping my own mouth. "You gave me an appetizer. I want the main course."

"Patience is a virtue," he said as he continued to work magic on my hand, turning it over and letting his lips press against the inside of my wrist. "Wouldn't you say that's true?" His tongue weaved a trail up to the inside of my elbow, making me realize that I had a new erogenous zone.

"I think patience is overrated." I pretended to pout, which actually did the trick. He met my mouth with his own and pressed his hips down toward mine. I felt his hardness against me and I wrapped my legs around his waist. His hand came up underneath me, pulling me closer toward him. I pressed his shirt upwards, hinting that he should remove it.

"You're serious?"

"Absolutely."

He shook his head at me, but smiled nonetheless as he lifted off his shirt, revealing a broad chest and toned abs that looked like a staircase that I definitely wanted to explore. In a word, he was amaaazing. Strong yet tender. I wanted him to hold me and let me tell him what he wanted to hear, but truth be told, I also wanted more from him. I wanted him to give up the missions, but that was something I would never ask of him. I wanted him home and safe.

I ran my hand lightly over his chest, slowly moving downward to rest lightly on the top button of his jeans. I paused long enough to meet his glance, and then with a raise of my eyebrow, I tugged and the five buttons of his 501s opened with little effort.

"I feel overdressed," I said indicating my workout outfit.

"You are most decidedly overdressed. Let me rectify this situation." Nate ran a finger lightly under the waist band of my yoga pants. It sent a chill down my spine and as he lowered them ever so slightly and bent his head to kiss the area he exposed, I audibly sighed. "It's a shame that my touch doesn't do anything for you."

"Yeah, nothing," I muttered.

He pulled my pants completely off and pressed his mouth to the outside of my panties. "These are nice," he said taking in the small scrap of white silk that was edged with black lace. "Something tells me you had this all planned."

"That's ridiculous. Who would plan to take you out to a deserted hiking trail just to have their way with you?"

"You would," he said linking his thumbs into the soft fabric. As he helped me shimmy out of them, he bent his head to my stomach, moving past my belly button and continuing to plant kisses over the protruding bone of my hip, following it to where my upper thigh bent at the joint. His tongue trailed over my flesh until it hovered just above where I needed it most.

His mouth parted the folds of my most intimate area and when his tongue ran lightly over me, it was electric. His hand worked it's way under my hips, gently pulling me toward him while he continued to kiss me there.

I sighed and looked up at the sky feeling amazed at how comfortable I was with Nate. "You know I wouldn't bring you here just so I could have my way with you," I murmured.

"Mmm hmm."

"I could have my way with you at home," I giggled in spite of the most amazing feeling that he was sending through my body.

And that's when Nate did the unexpected. He flipped me over and spanked me!

"Ouch."

He propped himself up on his elbows, his beautiful kissing having ceased and looked at me, waiting for an explanation. Stupid me. "Oops."

"Is that all you have to say?" he said, more amused than anything.

"Double oops?"

"You could try something like, 'Nate you are an amazing, warm-blooded, woodland creature that I am so lucky to have come across.'"

"Woodland creature?"

"With supernatural powers of seduction," he said moving his eyebrows up and down in a joking, creepy way. He ran his hands over my arms, warming me at his touch.

"Well, that goes without saying. So how about more?"

"More what?" he asked. His tone amused.

I moved closer and met his mouth with mine. Our kiss quickly intensified, our naked bodies once again pressing against each other. He was fun to tease, but I wasn't going to spoil this moment again no matter how tempting it was to have a go at him. I spoke against his mouth, never wanting to leave it. "I want more of you."

"I'm all yours," he said, and then we started the most beautiful dance, slowly moving against each other, every motion of mine matched by his own seductive waltz until we collapsed in each other's arms.

# # #

We never did take our hike. It was too luxurious to just bask in the sun, lying in each other's arms feeling totally free. There was always next weekend for hiking. This one was most decidedly destined for something else. I leaned over and gently kissed the tip of Nate's nose, waking him from a light slumber.

"We should get going," he said shielding his eyes from the sun above.

"Yeah, we're supposed to meet my sister and Zach for a light dinner. I forgot to tell you. Oh, and we're cooking."

"Good one. I guess we can grab stuff for spaghetti and meatballs on the way back." He stood up and offered his hand to me, easily pulling me to my feet. I took a deep breath of the fresh air, a welcome refuge from the city that was only thirty minutes away, but when out here in the middle of the wilderness it seemed miles away. Bending down to pick up the blanket, I suddenly felt the blood rush in my head, making me dizzy. I must have stumbled slightly as Nate immediately noticed.

"You okay?"

"Yeah, it was just a head rush."

"You want to sit for a bit?"

I shook my head. "I'm fine."

He took me in his arms and kissed the top of my head. "There's no hurry. You can persuade me to stay."

"Yeah, you'd like that. But...then I wouldn't beat you to the car!" I took off running.

"You! I'm going to get you!" he said chasing after me, trying to whip my butt with the blanket as I tore over the trail, making my way back to the highway where we left our car.

We reached the trail marker and our car completely breathless. "I won!"

"You cheated."

"What? That little head start?"

He opened the door for me and then walked around to the driver's side. Once we pulled back onto Mulholland Highway, I confessed, "I didn't have a very big breakfast. Probably why I only took you by a few yards."

He smiled at me. "That must be the reason."

Being with Nate was always like this...easy, fun, and everything about us just felt so right. Everything was perfect.

And then, the first motorcycle came speeding by the side of the car, nearly taking off the side mirror, and veering precariously in front of the car. "Jeez, someone's out for a Sunday drive," Nate muttered under his breath. The motorcyclist was followed by another, and then another. A band of about twenty leather clad bikers suddenly sped by on either side of our car, making both of us catch our breath.

"You know they look so tough, but most of them are doctors and lawyers during the week."

"How do you know?" I asked, my pulse only now returning to normal after the surprise onslaught of biker traffic.

"My dermatologist owns a Harley."

"No way."

"Yeah, he showed me a picture."

"No, I meant, you see a dermatologist? What for? Botox?"

"Funny." And then after a momentary beat, he quipped, "I have to...or people would think I'm robbing the cradle."

I wrinkled my nose and gave him a questioning look. "But you're only two years older than me."

"I'm talking maturity."

I loved our banter. Usually I hated when people teased me, but with Nate I knew he wouldn't feel comfortable doing so unless he loved me. In a word, the day was perfect.

I leaned over to kiss Nate on the cheek and he did that thing he does -- turning his head at the last minute so my lips met his, rather than just the scruff of his cheek. I saw the deer bound across the highway just a moment before Nate did.

I know I screamed, but the sound became mixed with the squeal of the tires as Nate turned the car suddenly. We fishtailed and spun in what felt like an endless circle until miraculously we came to a stop, albeit on the wrong side of the road. I looked out my window and to my relief, I saw the deer safely on the lower bank of the mountain, just staring at us as if to say, "What the ...."

We were safe. I exhaled and that's when the truck came around the blind curve, not expecting to find a car stationary on the wrong side of the two-lane highway. The driver instinctively blared his horn, a sound that melded with the nauseating sound of metal crushing on metal as it plowed into the driver's side at 45 miles per hour, carrying us along with it.

Chapter 6 - Nate

My head was throbbing; my body felt worse than it did when I used to play football and was called out to hold the blocking pad while half a dozen linebackers would take turns slamming their bodies into it while I accepted the impact. Basically, I felt like I had been hit by a truck. Oh yeah, I had. But at least the deer lived.

I couldn't quite open my eyes. Everything felt heavy and light at the same time. I strained to listen for Ella, trying to hear her breathing, but I couldn't. Forcing myself, I opened one eye and then slowly the other. Shit. Smashed windshield, the side nearest me was protruding inward practically wrapped around where I was harnessed in by the seatbelt. The car was a write-off.

"Ella?"

I couldn't turn my head. Nothing was working. It was too quiet. First, the sound of squealing tires, the barreling thundering noise of the truck's approach and now nothing.

"Ella?"

Damn it. Just say my name. Tell me you're alive. I needed to know that she was okay. Funny, beautiful Ella. The girl I loved with all my heart.

With more effort than I've ever put into anything before I turned my head to look to the side where she sat. Her head was propped against her side window and to my horror it was splattered with blood. Her blood. Please, please, please. I said the words over and over in my head. Willing her to look at me, to tell me she was alright.

A small moan sounded from her. "Ella?" I said her name again, weakly, but she heard it.

She opened her eyes, but her head slumped forward. With effort, she turned toward me. Our eyes met and I smiled with immense relief.

"Ella, you're okay." I fumbled to undo my seatbelt, shrugging it off. "I need to find help."

"Nate..."

"You're okay," I repeated. "I'm just going to..." suddenly it felt hard to speak again, but I had to find help. I had to help her.

"No, don't leave me!"

Her voice sounded different, stronger than it had only moments before. I took that to be a good thing.

"Nate, stay with me!"

"I'm going to find help. Ella...it'll be okay. Believe in me."

I saw her close her eyes again, and I knew that I had to hurry.

Chapter 7 - Ella

I felt so tired. It was good to just lie here for a moment with my eyes closed. I tried to breathe in the scent of the pine trees, but instead the smell of antiseptic accosted me. That's so strange. Maybe Nate's cleaning up. He's such a boy scout, always prepared for our hikes with his first aid kit.

"Her injuries are mild considering..."

"She looks so frail. When will she wake up?"

Is that Lily? What is my sister doing here and who is she talking to?

Again, the smell of clean struck me. Nate, why are they here? The question came to me, but the answer escaped my mind.

I heard a man's voice and it seemed as if he were speaking about me. "She was awake momentarily; that was earlier. She has a broken arm, two broken ribs, and a fairly serious concussion, which will need observation to ensure there isn't any swelling of the brain. Her lower extremities are fine, which is miraculous considering the way the side panels of the car were bent around her. No internal bleeding, either. She's lucky to be alive."

"When she was awake...did she seem..." Lily's voice trailed off.

What? What is she asking?

She spoke again, this time with her usual business-like clip. "Does she know about Nate?"

"When we delivered the news she became non-communicative, but that's to be expected after the trauma."

Silence ensued between the two of them. I felt someone take my hand. It was a light touch. The hand was too cold to be Nate's. His hand was always so warm and strong. I was safe with Nate. Nate. I really wanted to sleep.

"It's going to be okay, Ella." The sound of my sister's voice came to me again, which was sheer craziness because she hates to hike. Lily doesn't have an outdoorsy bone in her entire body. I tried imagining what reliable, practical Lily would say if she heard that Nate and I had made love outside in the woods. She'd probably worry about getting poisoned ivy on her back side. I felt a cool hand on my forehead. Her voice came to me again. "I love you, Ella."

That's so nice.

"You're going to stay with me for awhile."

What? You've got to be kidding. Me living with Lily? Why would I do that? Definitely not a dream...and I drifted back into the darkened quiet.

Chapter 8 - Nate

One Week Later...

Sweet Ella, you are so stubborn. But that's one of the things I love about you.
I watched as she struggled to put on the clothes that Lily had brought to her, refusing any help from the nurse. When she grabbed a hair brush, automatically picking it up with her left hand in spite of that arm being housed in a cast, she nearly whacked herself in the head with the plaster.
Ella, you're supposed to be getting out of the hospital, not causing yourself another concussion.
"Miss, are you sure you don't need any assistance?"
"I don't need anything." Her voice sounded clipped.
Chill Ella. She's just trying to be nice.
Ella's eyes met the nurse's concerned gaze. "I'm fine. Thank you."

"Okay then, I'll leave you to finish getting dressed. Your sister should be here soon."

"My sister?"

You're staying with her.

The nurse stared, concern washing over her expression again. "Your discharge papers have all been signed by the doctor, so whenever she gets here, you're free to go home."

"Her home," Ella's voice sounded disappointed, nervous, angry even.

The nurse touched her arm gently. "Give yourself time."

It'll be okay, Ella. I won't let anything bad happen to you. Your sister...so she's a little uptight, but she means well. And Zach, he's cool. My bud. He balances her.

Ella nodded, more to herself than the nurse who left her after offering a comforting pat on her shoulder.

# # #

Lily's place was always much neater than Ella's, but now I finally know her secret. She has her own dumping ground. That amazing thing called a spare room that is actually the place where everything that doesn't have a purpose or place is stashed.

Watching her and Zach clean away the clutter, separating the items into piles for either charity, friends, garbage or "to be determined" -- meaning the things that would be moved to a new dumping ground in her garage -- was like watching an episode of "House Hoarders."

"Zach, she wouldn't even talk to me. First, losing our parents last year and now Nate. He was her rock. What if..." before she could finish her thoughts, the tears started to flow.

Zach stood rather awkwardly, balancing his weight back and forth between his two feet.

Come on, buddy. Don't just stand there like some wind-up soldier.

Zach opened his arms and Lily willingly walked into his embrace, burying her face into his shoulder.

"Thanks."

"It'll take time."

Lily nodded, a gesture that seemed to be more directed at convincing herself of the sentiment rather than agreeing with Zach, and then turned her attention back to packing. She reached for a cluster of romance paperbacks, stopping to admire the covers of each one, before placing them in one of her "to keep" boxes. As her hand graced a large scrapbook, she sat down on the bed and called Zach over.

"Do you remember this day?" she asked pointing to a photo.

A smile crept up on Zach's face. "The four of us at Disneyland."

"Nate's birthday."

"They gave him that button to wear that said, 'It's my birthday!'"

Zach nodded, remembering the day, and Lily broke out in a sudden giggle.

You all had way too much fun at my expense on that day.

"He kept forgetting he was wearing the button and then random strangers would wish him a happy birthday."

"And the characters would come up and hug him," Lily added with a smile.

"Ella tried to get a picture with him next to every Disney princess," Zach laughed.

"Yeah, that was a good day." Lily added, the momentary laughter now dying out of her.

The awkward silence ensued with neither one saying the obvious...

No more birthdays for me, folks. But you guys have to focus on Ella. Take care of her.

Lily snapped out of it first, back to working at the task at hand, sending items into boxes. "I need to finish this up and get some of Ella's favorites before picking her up."

"I'll finish this up," he said taping up another box. "I'll drop these off at charity, and then I'll come by tomorrow."

"Want to stay for dinner?"

"You should spend the night with Ella alone."

"You sure?"

"I'll come by in the morning. I'll bring breakfast."

Lily raised up on her toes and kissed Zach on the chin before grabbing her purse and heading out.

Chapter 9 - Ella

We drove in silence. Awkward silence. I loved my sister, but we never had a ton in common, even though we hung out as much as possible. But somehow, our outings always ended with her doling out advice. I suppose it's a big sister thing and evidence that she cares, but I can't handle it now.

I'm tired of hearing people tell me that everything will be okay when things are so not alright. Not even close. The pain in my heart is overwhelming. And yet, I can't cry. It's almost as if it hurts too much for mere tears. Tears are what happens to me when I watch a Richard Curtis movie like "Bridget Jones' Diary" and she realizes that her boyfriend likes her "just the way she is."

Nate loved me just as I am. In spite of all my foibles, he loved me. Heck, he even found my idiosyncrasies appealing, cute. He never tried to change me. He was the Mr. Darcy to my messed up Bridget.

"In time..." Lily started to speak, but I shot her a look and she immediately thought better of the sentiment that was about to escape her mouth.

More cliché words. Time heals. You have to move on with your life. In the last week, the hospital psych ward had rattled off all of those tried and true statements, waiting for my acceptance of them. So, I gave them what they wanted. My agreement. It was the fastest way for my discharge papers to be signed and for me to escape the constant physical and mental prodding that occurred in that sterile environment.

What I didn't need was to start it all over again at the hands of my sister.

"Don't," I said quietly, breaking the silence in the car.

"Don't what? I just want to help you."

"I don't want anybody's help. I don't even know why you're taking me to your place."

"Because it's just...better."

"I don't see how that's possible. I'm an adult, capable of taking care of myself," I said and then accidentally knocked the window with my cast as I tried to rub a spot underneath my sweater, where the tape that was wrapping my broken ribs was making my skin feel raw.

Lily sent me an "I told you so" look and turned onto a street marked by an unmanned guardhouse erected next to a set of double gates that looked far more ostentatious than the homes on the other side required.

She opened her window and punched a four-digit code on a keypad and waited momentarily for the gates to open. Each house was painted in soothing earth tones, alternating between three different styled models. Lily turned down the first street, continued to the house on the end, the smaller of the three home styles within the gates, and pulled her car into the driveway.

I looked outside the window and braced myself for the conversation that would no doubt ensue. What did I want for dinner? What did I want to do tomorrow? How she could meet my basic needs while avoiding the conversation that I really wanted to have -- how would I ever live without Nate?

I decided to head her off at the pass. "You've done a lot with the place."

"Thanks. Zach and I have been trying to do up the garden. You know, give it more street appeal."

"It's working," I said politely.

"I guess. It's the smallest model, but they say in terms of investment, it's better to buy the most modest house on the block rather than the grandest."

I nodded absently. I wasn't in the mood to talk investments because it would invariably be an opening for Lily to ask me what I was doing with my life. My career, actually...I couldn't even use that word...my job is a more accurate description because nobody would make a career out of being a fact checker. The job earned me a small siphon compared to Lily's more promising future as a paralegal. She was bound for law school before our parents died, but I had no doubt that she would still get there. She just had to take a side step in her life's plans. I took a deep breath before stepping out of the car, wondering what sort of indirect route my life's navigation system had planned for me.

I followed Lily through the garage and into the house. Neat as always. Flowers on the table. Magazines perfectly splayed out on the coffee table, like at a doctor's office. I took a moment to look at her offerings on display: "Modern Home," "Time Magazine," "Forbes." Not a "People" or "Us" in sight. Well, that was probably a good thing. I didn't need to read about how another celebrity couple had split up after a cheating episode. I certainly didn't need to read about a star-studded marriage. I just needed a bed so that I could go to sleep.

"You okay?"

"Yeah, can I go to...?"

"Your room?"

"Sure. Yes, my room."

"Second door on the right," she pointed down the hallway. "I'm just going to make sure that Zach put the towels in the bathroom for you. He was helping me get the place ready," she explained.

When Lily returned she stared at me just standing awkwardly in the middle of the room. "Try out the bed," she suggested.

I looked at the bed suddenly realizing that Lily had never had a bed in her guest room. She had always used it as more of an extra room for studying. "When did you get a bed?"

"Zach brought it from your place...so it would feel more like home to you."

"I wish you hadn't gone to so much trouble."

"You're my sister. You're not any trouble. Besides, it looks better like this. I also went to your place to get some of your clothes," she added, as if giving credence to my original comment.

I nodded. "That was nice of you," I answered, if not a bit forced.

Lily left me and I let my eyes drift over "my room." My clothes were neatly laid out on the bed. She had even thought to bring my kindle over, and my diary.

I sat down on the bed and ran my finger over my diary's cover, a garish display of pink rhinestones that lined the edges with the words, "Inner Most Thoughts," printed in silver glitter in the center. Lily had given it to me earlier this year on my birthday. I smiled remembering how she told me that she wanted to do something artistic for me. Her attempt landed her in the emergency room after she super glued her fingers together. I smiled at the memory and opened my book to a random page.

But sobs arrived, fast and uncontrollable. My fingers had found the one and only page that Nate had written on. One day, he insisted that he had an "inner most thought" that had to be shared and he grabbed the book and retreated into the bathroom with it.

"You better not do a stinky in there with it," I had told him. He emerged fifteen minutes later, holding the diary page wide open to show an intricate cartoon with the first frame showing cupid shooting an arrow straight into the heart of a man that was obviously meant to be a self-portrait. The second frame showed a light bulb above the man's head and then it ended in the final frame, with the man farting out hearts, the words, "I love you!" in a balloon above his head.

"The bathroom inspired me," he had said when I spied the final scene.

The cries that wouldn't come now hit me uncontrollably. Loud and hard the sounds of my anguish poured out of my soul. My sister ran down the hall and came into my room, seeing my hands gripping the diary.

"Here," she said gently putting it down on the bed. "Come here," she said and opened her arms to me.

For once, she didn't say anything. She just held me and let me cry into her shoulder. She rubbed my back gently and just let me be.

Chapter 10 - Nate

Ella had barely eaten in two days. Her breakfast consisted of coffee, but she wasn't even enjoying that the way she used to. Gone were the puddles of half and half and spoonfuls of sugar. Instead, she tried to drink it down black as if relishing the bitterness of the liquid that now matched her mood.

Although Lily was doing her best, her efforts to help were more maternal than that of a sister or friend. Ella retreated to her room to find solitude from the well intentioned advice Lily doled out. She would emerge for meals, but merely shift the food around on her plate not touching any of it. She was gaunt and pale, and although the lack of food had made her lethargic, sleep escaped her. When it did come it was sporadic and plagued by nightmares of the crash. The fact that the police had questioned her repeatedly, engraining the details of the accident in her mind, surely hadn't helped matters.

I hated seeing her like this. She was my world -- a petite brunette with a waist so small I could wrap my arms clear around her until I could touch my own elbows. I would do anything to hold her now and ease her suffering. Hell, I'd hold onto her every moment if I could. I wanted to keep her safe, but most of all, I just wanted to smell the perfume that was her hair, feel the softness that was her skin, and drink in every bit of her.

But what I loved most about Ella was that she kept me on my feet. She could drink me under the table and I'm sure if I entered a pie-eating contest or something similar, she'd put me to shame. For all her outward daintiness, she was still one of the guys. The only time this wasn't ideal was during sleep. Then, she might as well have been a football linebacker.

Her presence in bed was always known. Not one to tiptoe quietly and settle down, she plopped, sighed, and then the snoring ensued. She never stayed close to the edge of the bed. Ella was all about the center. I watched her now, sprawled out smack in the middle, and if I had been with her I would have loved feeling her nudge herself into my space. I wanted to hold her now to ease her troubled mind.

She may have been plagued by nightmares tonight, but she still looked beautiful. Would it be so wrong if I just let her feel some comfort from my presence? If I was able to see her, then perhaps I could help...if only for awhile. She thrashed against the mattress and held on tightly to the pillow. She should be at peace. She should be holding me.

I knew it was risky and I couldn't honestly say that I was doing this solely for Ella. The desire to hold her one last time was so strong that I slid into bed next to her and drew the covers up around us. The mattress sagged in that familiar way whenever I came to bed, causing Ella to slide toward me. It was the reason I never wanted to get a new mattress. This one had advantages, lumps and all. I silently thanked Zach for lugging it over here.

As she slid into me, her breathing settled and she rested her head against my chest, the way she always did. Her head fitting perfectly in the crook between my collarbone and my chin, resting against my neck as if she were made to fit into that spot. I smelled the flower scent of her hair and wrapped my arms around her, and her arm instinctively moved over my chest.

She sighed, peace coming to her at last. That was good. That's all I wanted. Maybe this wasn't wrong.

But then Ella threw her leg over my body to match the ease of which her arm rested against me. This was no dream, at least not for me. Her thigh brushed against my cock. I inhaled sharply, willing her to settle and just curl up next to me in sleep, but she kept it in place. Feeling her press against me was agony and pleasure wrapped in one. I focused on why I was here and remembered how distraught she had been the last two nights when sleep finally came to her. If I could bring her a few memories, a bit of happiness, then she could sleep in peace. So I let her keep that magnificent thigh, one of many parts of her that tortured my thoughts, against my ever growing hardness and wrapped a protective arm around her back.

"Mmm, Nate..."

Hell, that sleepy morning voice always got me. Ella pressed her hips firmer against my leg. My hand automatically drifted downward, coming to rest on her bottom. She stirred under my touch and moved her hips against my leg again as she murmured my name once more.

"Oh Nate, do you want me?"

Fuck yes.

But this was just a dream for Ella. For me, it was reality. This wasn't working out the way I had intended. I had hoped to just bring her a little comfort, offer a warm embrace that would allow her to sleep longer and enjoy the respite of not thinking about me. Time and sleep could heal her troubled mind, I rationalized. This wasn't supposed to end up with her thinking about me more. I never thought that I would get so caught up in feeling her next to me. I needed to resist her.

But then I heard her soft moan, a damn sexy moan, I might add. It escaped her beautiful mouth as she ran her hand over her own body. "That's nice," she mumbled. As she touched herself, her arm also brushed against me. She moved her hand upwards from her bent knee up to the curve of her waist and then to her breast. Sandwiched together, I felt every touch.

I gently lifted my head, careful not to cause the mattress to move or wake her. Good news...she was asleep. Better news...she was having a damn good dream about me and her whispered voice mumbled, "God, I want you."

Which brought me to the bad news...I wanted her right back.

This wasn't real. I was dead. For all I knew, I was the one dreaming, not her. So what was the harm, really? She's finally enjoying sleep. Thinking about me like this is certainly an improvement over remembering the accident and the hospital. I rolled over onto my side and she did the same so we were facing each other. Our hips touched and my breath hitched as she pressed against me.

She furrowed her brow ever so slightly as if her subconscious heard me inhale sharply. I released my hand from where it had come to rest on the small of her back and didn't move a muscle. She snuggled up closer to me as if willing memories of us together to continue. To leave her would surely cause her to wake and given the expression on her face, which was quickly returning to troubled, I could argue that it was best to remain close to her. But to stay would mean a line was crossed and I couldn't...shouldn't.

Yet, she smelled so good. She felt warm and inviting. She slid her hand against my groin and that's when the seesaw that had become my brain swayed to the side of being with her.

I grew hard once again under her touch. She moved her hand, allowing it to caress herself and me at the same time given the way our bodies rested next to each other.

"Touch me."

Damn. How I wanted to. But whatever reprieve I was giving her mind, not to mention her body, could all go by the wayside if I went and woke her. Whereas before I was debating if I should go with this crazy dream, now I wondered just how far I could take it without waking her. Talk about pressure.

But when she turned her hand over and fully cupped my cock, instinct took over and this time, it was my mind that was given a rest. Gone was any internal struggle of my conscience. I was all hers as she moved her hand up and down the length of me. Without any more hesitation, I wrapped my arm around her back once more, pulled her against me and relished in the feeling of her leg wrapped around mine. I let my hand trail up her side, coming to rest on her breast. My thumb gently ran over her nipple and then I bent my head and took it in my mouth.

"Mmmm," she laid her head back against the pillow and I slowly trailed kisses around her breast and then up her neck, along her jaw and then her hands found their way into my hair and she was pulling my head toward hers.

My mouth found hers and I moved atop her, my legs shimmying between hers. The kiss was sweet and soft. But the way her hips moved upward against mine was beyond hot. Her nightie slipped up as she pushed against me once more. My hand went to the soft silk of her panties and I lightly touched her between her legs.

"Oh Nate," she repeated again in her sleep. But this time, her voice wasn't a mere whisper. I heard the footsteps coming down the hall.

"Shh," I whispered gently. Still holding her, I once again trailed kisses down her neck. "You're going to be alright. I love you, Ella."

Ella opened her eyes only seconds before the door swung open.

"Are you okay?" Lily looked at her with concern.

Ella looked around the room as if being woken from her dream made her question its reality. It seemed so real.

"Yeah, I'm sorry if I woke you," Ella said hesitantly, still looking slightly freaked out.

"Nah, I've been up. But you were talking in your sleep."

Ella's expression changed to nervousness and embarrassment. "What did you hear?" she asked tentatively.

"Just you, calling for Nate," Lily said gently and crossed to the bed. "Will you come and join me for breakfast? Maybe actually eat something today?"

"Sure. Toast?"

"You got it. You look like you actually got some sleep."

Ella let a small smile cross her lips. "Yeah, a little."

Lily smiled back, but concern crossed her features as if she hated to ruin the moment. Finally, Ella had agreed to eat, had slept, but it had to be said... "Ella? Today is..."

Ella's smile quickly vanished as she remembered. Today was my funeral.

"I'll go...make coffee," Lily said before retreating out the door.

Ella flopped back down onto the mattress, letting her hand brush against the spot next to her where I had laid just moments earlier. Her eyes opened wider as she realized the spot was warm. She closed her eyes immediately, willing her mind to feel what it had just a minute ago rather than focus on the day ahead of her.

She remembered my hands, my mouth. Ella inhaled deeply, allowing herself to feel the momentary happiness as well as the fleetingness of the memory all at once.

Chapter 11 - Ella

Nate always thought I looked sexy in black. I crossed my legs and when my skirt drifted upwards slightly revealing the tops of my thigh high stockings, I didn't bother to push it back down. Nate loved thigh highs. He would appreciate me wearing them today to his... My mind reeled with the word...funeral. It was surreal. How could he be dead? He was my everything. He couldn't leave me. And crazy as it sounded, maybe he didn't.

Last night was the first time I had slept in the week since the accident. I felt him. Boy, did I feel him. I closed my eyes trying to recall the sensation of his touch. It seemed so real. Logically, I knew it had to have been a dream, but that was one dream that I hoped to relive again soon. It made me feel like Nate was here with me. I took a deep breath and then felt Lily's arm move over my shoulders, jarring me out of the memory.

She was only trying to help. Like always. She probably saw me sitting here with my eyes closed, breathing deeply and thought I was going to lose it. If she only knew that I was trying to recall how it felt to wrap my hand over Nate's... then she would be sure I had lost it. And maybe she would be right. But I didn't care. That dream made me alive again, and for the first time I wasn't wishing that I had left this world too. People are so quick to say that one should get on with their life. That was the last thing I wanted to do.

I still had a couple bits of dirty laundry that Nate had worn. Lily had tried to pry them off me, but I wouldn't let her. Tonight that dirty shirt was going to find its way under my pillow. It wasn't dirty as in sweaty, but it smelled of Nate. His sweet, musky scent that filled me and made me remember. How I wanted to remember everything about him. And last night I did.

"Ella? You coming?"

I turned toward Lily, who was already standing. The men holding Nate's casket had already turned and were heading outdoors to where the rest of the service would continue...to where Nate would be placed in his final resting spot. No, I didn't want to go there.

Zach was among them and he turned to catch my eye. He gave me a small nod as if to say, "It would be okay." Lily was lucky to have him. He was a good friend to Nate, too.

"Yeah," I said to Lily. "I'm ready."

The sun was shining when they lowered the casket into the ground. The clergyman said something about the weather and its testament to Nate's sunny disposition. People dabbed their eyes. I stared without seeing the world around me. The men in suits. The white flowers in contrast to the dark wood of the casket. Just like the funeral that I had attended with Nate only two weeks earlier. The irony of the situation wasn't lost on me. He had survived fighting and bombings in Afghanistan only to lose his life because we went on a stupid hike.

So many 'maybes' filled my mind. Maybe if we had left earlier rather than fall asleep. Maybe if we hadn't made love we wouldn't have fallen asleep at all. And the worst one...maybe if I had just said yes to his proposal we wouldn't have been on that highway. We may have been planning our future together.

The sound of baby birds chirping brought my mind back to the ceremony outdoors. It was a normally cheerful sound that today made me sad, realizing that I wouldn't have babies with Nate. More irony. More indications that I was losing my mind. I could listen to the entire service without shedding a tear and now the sound of nature caused me to blubber. I missed our hikes, but I wondered if I could ever go back there. A continual flood of random thoughts that had nothing to do with this particular moment assaulted my brain.

Lily held my hand and I squeezed hers back, thankful that she was here and always so strong and capable.

"People are coming back to the house. Can you handle it?"

I nodded, wondering when she had made all of the arrangements and chiding myself for being so out of it.

"I'm sorry that I haven't helped you. I should have been the one to do it."

"Nonsense. You just got out of the hospital. You've been through hell. His mom did all of this," she motioned with her chin to the mound of dirt in front of us. "I just called the deli."

I gave her a half smile, knowing that I hadn't done anything except stay in my room for the past week. "Still. It's nice of you. Nate would have liked it -- being at your house."

She nodded. "You ready? Zach is calling us to the car."

I looked up and saw him waving us over, so we headed down the grassy hill, my high heels sinking into the grass with each step. At least I could aerate the soil. I was good for something.

# # #

The gathering at the house was everything Nate would have wanted. People ate, talked, sat around longer than they should have for fear of leaving the grieving to their thoughts. He loved a party and enjoyed having people around. Myself, on the other hand, couldn't wait to be alone again. Alone so that I could be with Nate. Please let me find him again.

I started to clear away the paper plates and surreptitiously packed away bits of food into ziplock baggies. I didn't want Lily to do everything, I reasoned. Besides, the longer it was out, the longer they would all stay.

"You're putting away the food while people are still here," Lily chided.

"I just don't want anyone to get food poisoning."

Lily placed a gentle hand on my shoulder. "I think people are starting to clear out."

I nodded, hoping that her observation was correct. It was just too hard to talk to people as if my world hadn't come shattering down on me. I know the gathering is meant to bring people together in comfort, but for me, it was a reminder of why everyone was here...because Nate died. If they would all just leave, I could focus on his life again. I could remember him...and maybe, I could find him again, at least in my mind.

When the last person left, I immediately went down the hall to my room.

"Are you going to bed?" Lily called out.

"Yeah," I said over my shoulder, hardly stopping to answer.

"You want to watch T.V. with us?" Zach offered.

I couldn't be rude after all that they were doing for me. "That's okay. You guys deserve some time alone." I could see Zach wrapping his arms around Lily's waist and nuzzling her neck.

Lily elbowed him. "Ella, we don't mind. You'll like this movie."

Zach straightened up reminding me of a teenager who had been caught trying to cop a feel for his girlfriend. "Yeah, come on Ella. I'll make popcorn."

"It's really okay. I ate a ton," I added, thinking it would make Lily happy. It only caused her to raise her eyebrows at me in a 'sure you did' way. "Good night."

"Good night, Ella," they said in unison.

# # #

The clock on my nightstand read 1:45. I stared at it in frustration. I wanted sleep to take me so desperately. I wanted the dream to come to me again. I flipped my pillow, straightened the covers around me and once again settled in, but I just felt uncomfortable and unable to relax. I tried with all my might to remember the way it felt to hold Nate, but it was already slipping away.

I turned to look at the bottle of painkillers on my nightstand. It was prescribed while I was in the hospital and at the time, I wanted to feel the pain. But now, I wanted to wash it away. I reasoned if I could just sleep, then maybe I could see Nate again. I shook out one pill, swallowed it without the help of water, and relaxed as my mind turned to Jell-O mush.

# # #

"Hey, you're up early," Lily looked up in surprise as I came into the kitchen. "And you're dressed."

"Going to work today."

"Already? You sure?"

"Yeah, I can't just keep moping around," I said pouring myself a cup of coffee. The remnants of the pain medicine still had my brain feeling fuzzy. I still skipped my usual healthy helping of brown sugar, but relented when Lily handed me the half and half.

"I just thought that maybe we could do something today," she offered.

"Lily, you need to get back to work too. Really, I'll be fine. I might even go back to my apartment."

"No," she said a bit quicker than I expected. I gave her a surprised look. "Ella, just take it slow. You've been through a horrible trauma. You're lucky to have walked away from that accident. Not to mention, what you're going through having lost..." her voice trailed off and for that, I was thankful. I couldn't bear to hear her say the obvious, that I had lost Nate. "Ella, please, just come back here after work. At least for a bit longer."

I nodded. "I'll see you around 6. Do you want me to pick up something for dinner?"

"I've got it. Just...just take care of yourself."

"I'll be fine," I insisted, and grabbed my purse and headed out the door.

# # #

Driving to work felt different today. I mean, obviously it would. I hadn't been in for two weeks, but it felt familiar and yet odd all at once. I passed the Starbucks where Nate and I would meet for coffee.

The grocery store where we shopped. The street with the pretty blue house we both admired and hoped to buy one just like it...someday.

I pulled into the underground garage of work, thankful that I would be sitting in a boring office where there was nothing to remind me of happiness, enjoyment or Nate. Being a fact checker for an online magazine had to be the most boring of jobs, but I had finally found the silver lining to it.

My walk down the long corridor to where my desk was located, one of four that stood outside the editor's offices, was usually uneventful. Today, I couldn't take one step without setting off some sort of silent alarm that warned people to come out of their office and take pity on me. Everyone wanted to give me their condolences. And each person who came out from behind their desk wore the same sad expression. It was a mixture of grief and something else...a look that said they were thankful that their own lives hadn't changed. Three weeks ago each one of them had left their desk on a Friday night, enjoyed the weekend and returned Monday morning. Sure, they may have complained about the monotony of their lives, but now in seeing me they were secretly thankful for it.

I got that. I wanted it too. So I nodded my head, smiled politely to every well-wisher and thankfully sank into my swivel chair and twirled it around so that my back faced the wall of offices where the pity looks gathered and I could just convene with my computer screen.

I remained in that position, never looking up, never taking a coffee break until lunch time when I went outside to the park where I ate my first bite of food of the day -- a pretzel from a man with a cart -- and forced down the chewy blandness before turning around and going right back to my desk. I didn't need a break. The last thing I wanted was an opportunity to clear my mind. What I needed was the endless articles and names, numbers and locales. There were more facts than anyone could ever get through in a lifetime, but I was well on my way. I relished the distraction and stayed completely focused on my task until most of my co-workers had left for the day. I didn't want to go down the elevator with anyone. That would only serve to bring about more polite chit-chat or sorrowful glances.

I reached into my purse, searching for the pain killers that were doing wonders to dull my senses. I didn't need dinner or conversation. All I needed was to get home and go to sleep.

Chapter 12 - Nate

Everything I thought I knew about death was wrong. It wasn't painful. It caused no pain. It was, in fact, peaceful...except for those left behind. If only I could talk to her. I would tell her that I'm alright. I would tell her that it's okay to forget me...or at least to go on without me.

I touched Ella's face ever so softly while she slept and instantly a deep sigh escaped her beautiful mouth and her worried look dissipated. Her sleep had been so restless. The house was cold and she had left her window open as if to bring more misery and discomfort to her life. I tentatively placed my hand on her and was shocked at the coldness of her skin.

Her body shook in spite of the blanket that covered her. It couldn't hurt to warm her, to make her more comfortable so she could sleep more soundly. It worked before and if careful, I could make her think it was just a dream again. Ever so gently, I crept into bed beside her and pulled her into my arms. She immediately cradled her body next to mine. I wrapped my arms around her and we spooned. Her lungs filled deeply and as she exhaled, I felt her body relax against mine. She lay without tossing for the first time in hours.

Until, the dream became too real...until she felt my presence. Her back was pressed against my chest, but she suddenly turned so that she was right up against me. Her head rested against my chest and she whispered my name. She shivered suddenly and I wrapped my arms around her, pulling her in close.

In spite of popular mythology about ghosts, I was able to give off heat. Her body warmed against mine. She held me tighter, pulling herself as close as possible to me as if fearful that the dream would end. She tilted her head upward, her eyes still closed in sleep. I felt bolder than I had the other night. Just like her, I had a taste for what it was like to be together again, and I didn't know if I would be able to resist her tonight.

It felt so good to hold her. I was doing it to keep her warm and offer solace, but I'd be lying if I didn't admit how good it felt to me too. Like a teenager, I started counting backwards, willing myself not to get too excited so I that I was satisfied in just being here for her, giving without receiving.

My touch was light, nearly undetectable and yet, comforting. Perhaps too comforting. Her head instinctively tilted up toward mine and then her mouth was now upon my own. There was no way I could resist her. My lips pressed against hers and she responded, wrapping her leg around mine, feeling just right. We fit. We always did.

"I miss you. Tell me you're here," she said and no sooner had she spoken the words, but her tongue found mine and weaved into my mouth. Being with her felt the way it always had and without thinking I moved my hand to her breast as I had so many nights before. I got caught up in the seduction and moved the way I normally would, forgetting that this wasn't the norm. I dipped my head lower and let my kisses line her neck.

"I'm here," I whispered against her throat.

Shit. I did not just say that.

Ella immediately was pulled from her dream, her eyes met mine and she stared as if, well, as if seeing a ghost.

Chapter 13 - Ella

"Oh my god, Nate."

The tears started to flow down my cheeks, but he lightly brushed them away with his hand, and then his mouth, kissing each one away until the sorrowful flow stopped. "Nate, please tell me this is real."

I refused to close my eyes for fear that the wonderful illusion of lying in bed with Nate would disappear. Instead, I leaned forward and pressed my lips to his, desperate to feel him.

His hands pressed against my back and his arms closed in, pulling me tighter.

"It's real, baby," he said against my mouth.

"How?"

Our eyes met and he ran his thumb along my cheek, once again wiping away a wayward tear. He tenderly smoothed the mess that was my hair, wild from nights of tossing and turning and days of not giving a damn.

"I don't know. I feel so alive, but I can't be. I'm here, but then I'm not. I watch you and when you're in pain, I so desperately want to take care of you. In those moments, I'm able to be here."

I placed both of my hands along Nate's cheeks and touched my forehead to his. I inhaled deeply, trying to capture his scent. It was the only thing that was fading from my memory and I wanted it back. I wanted all of him back. But trying to capture his scent was the only clue that something was still amiss. My room was growing light with the morning dawn and as the sun rose, so did my anxiety. I suddenly feared that I would lose him all over again.

"I don't want you to go. Not ever. Not again," I said emphatically.

"You're going to be okay, Ella. You have to believe that."

"I won't be. I don't want to be...not if that means living without you."

Once again I felt the tingle of his touch as he ran his hands up my arms and then soothingly stroked my hair. I placed my head against his chest, trying to listen for a heartbeat, but coming up empty. Still, it felt right lying there with him. I snuggled my cheek into the crook of his neck and relaxed against him.

"Just lay back against me and close your eyes," he said. His voice was soothing and sexy, and given his condition, it was surprisingly alive and strong. It was his military voice, the one that commanded attention and told me to listen. But I wasn't one of his new recruits ready to be dispatched to an assignment. This conversation couldn't be over.

"Wait. I need to tell you something. I should have told you before...when you asked..."

His voice became a faint whisper. "Sleep. You look exhausted."

"Thanks a lot."

"Don't worry. You're still beautiful."

"You'll be here when I wake up?" I fought the pull of sleep, but it was too strong.

"I'm always with you," I heard him say before I lapsed back into the darkness of my mind, but comforted that I fell asleep in Nate's arms.

# # #

I felt him. Heck, I *saw* him. Nate was with me. It couldn't have been just a dream. Then again, I had to go and blow it by waking up or falling asleep. At this point I wasn't sure which one. I only knew that I felt certain that I could reach him.

I stared up at the ceiling for a moment. For the first time since the accident, I didn't feel like a part of me had died in that car along with Nate. I felt hope. It was possible to be with him. But it was clear to me that these momentary dreams, or whatever they were...visits perhaps...just weren't enough. I needed more. I wanted him back and as crazy as it sounded, I was starting to think that I had found a way.

It was Sunday, our hiking day. I bounded out of bed, feeling a burst of energy that comes with having a plan and a purpose. I threw on my yoga pants, a t-shirt and running shoes, and then brushed my hair into a high ponytail.

I bounded into the kitchen catching Zach and Lily in one of their perpetual lip locks. For the first time, I didn't feel jealous or the need to turn away.

Lily jumped apart from Zach, obviously still feeling the need to pretend that she wasn't getting it every night while I lay alone and grieving.

"Stop it," I chided her. "It's okay to have a boyfriend. Tell her, Zach," I said smiling.

Zach gently tugged on my ponytail. "Morning, kiddo. Do you want some coffee?"

"Please," I said and moved to the cupboard to get out my jar of brown sugar. I caught Lily's interested stare out of the corner of my eye.

"You're going back to sugar?"

"I'm realizing that there's enough bitterness in life. It seemed silly to add to it by drinking my coffee black."

"You going running?" Zach asked. "It's kind of early."

"Actually, I'm going hiking."

It took about a nano second for both Lily and Zach to protest my idea.

If the fact that I already had an overprotective older sister wasn't enough, Zach put his hands on his hips, looking very much like an older brother. The last thing I needed was another sibling to watch over me.

"I don't think that's a good idea," Lily complained.

Zach seconded her thoughts. "It's a bit soon for that."

"Definitely too soon," Lily added.

"Listen, it's been four weeks since..." I couldn't bring myself to say it, so I just carried on my thought, "since...anyway. You've been saying that I don't eat, I don't sleep, I'm anti-social, I just stay in my room. So, I'm going out. And, I'm drinking breakfast," I said holding up my mug to them.

"Hardly the breakfast of champions," Zach noted dryly. "Listen Ella, Nate was my best friend. I just feel that he would want me to look after you."

"You have been looking after me. I just want some fresh air. It's nothing more than that. Don't read so much into it." The lie escaped my lips easily. It's not like I could tell them that Nate had been appearing to me in dreams and we had a hiking date.

They would think I was crazy, ready to be committed. And maybe I was because Nate hadn't actually told me to go hiking, but the draw of getting to the mountains was so strong, that in my heart, I felt like it was the right thing to do. I needed to believe in it.

"You won't be gone long?" Lily asked, her eyes still holding a worried expression.

"I promise." Not wanting to wait around for them to second guess me again, I grabbed a water bottle from the counter, my car keys, and headed out the door.

It was Sunday. Our day. There was no time to waste.

Chapter 14 - Nate

Ella ran like there was no tomorrow. She was always good at keeping up with me, but there was a common sense that never escaped her and kept her from taking risks. My training always gave me a leg up when it came to traversing the rough terrain of Red Rock Canyon with its steep hills and rocky paths. Today, had I been racing Ella, I'm not sure I could have taken her.

It worried me to see her so reckless, not just with her run, but with her entire body. She looked thin and tired, but persevered running toward the woods in spite of the strain that showed on her face.

"Ella, be careful."

She stopped suddenly and cocked her head to the side. She looked skyward as if wondering whether the sound of my voice was real or imagined. When she slowed her approach and finally reached the wooded area at the bottom of the trail head, I appeared. Tentatively at first, my image was that of a shadow. And then, when I was sure that she wouldn't spook from the sight of me, my form became more solid.

"You're here," she said, relief flooding her face.

I held out my arms and even stumbled a step back when she ran at me, plunging her body into mine with all of her force. She didn't hold anything back, coming at me with a running jump and then wrapping her legs around my waist. That's how I held her and then ever so slowly, allowed her to slide down my body and meet me in a kiss.

It was the most beautiful moment, not just because the early sun was just peeking behind the trees, but because I was with her. A multitude of shadows cast from the wintery limbs of the trees that extended to the ground, making it look like a zigzag maze for us to get lost in.

"Where's my latte?" I joked.

"Next time," she promised.

I took her hand and we walked through the woods, taking in the sounds of our solitude.

"Listen."

"To what? It's so quiet. It's perfect. This is the only place where I don't hear that horrible sound -- the crash."

"Shh," I squeezed her hand. "Just listen."

We continued through the woods together, making our way around the back side of the trail head to where it wrapped back around toward the highway. Our shoes sloshed through the mud, baby birds chirped in expectation of their morning feeding, and all around the leaves rustled with a hush.

She looked up at me. "Can we sit for a moment?"

How could I deny her anything, especially when she seemed the happiest that I had seen her in weeks? We found a clearing where the ground was firm and I lay down right there on top of a pile of soft leaves. I relished in the feeling of Ella lying next to me, resting her head on my chest, my arm wrapped protectively around her.

In spite of the sunshine, the January morning was crisp. Her body, now so thin from weeks of neglect, shivered involuntarily.

"Are you okay? We can walk again to warm up," I suggested.

"I don't want to. I just want you to hold me."

Ella propped herself up on her elbows and looked into my eyes, then ran her hand through my hair. I reached up for her and took her face in my hands and gently led her toward me. Our kiss wasn't filled with the urgency that it was on our last walk when we daringly made love in the woods. This time, it was slow and thoughtful, and filled with the need to draw it out and make it last.

I ran my tongue over her lips and my hands through her hair. She responded and allowed her mouth to leave mine, trailing her tongue and more delightful kisses down my neck. I relaxed my head back against the earth, relishing the way her lips felt over me. There were not enough minutes in time to make me feel as if I had spent enough of them with Ella. I could have stayed like that for as long as she wanted, but the wind changed and with it, I heard the sound of approaching footsteps.

Without warning, Ella took off running, chasing a shadow of myself that transformed into that of the tall trees. It's a cruel trick of the eye, but one that I can't seem to help. I wish I could stay longer, but something called me away. Searching for me, she continues to run and my heart catches in my throat when I hear the blare of a car horn and the swerve of tires against pavement.

"I love you, Ella. Be safe."

And then the sun passed behind the trees, casting long shadows along the ground, announcing my departure once again.

Chapter 15 - Ella

No! Why did he have to come and spoil everything? This was my place with Nate. It didn't belong to anyone else. Now, some random jogger decides to start a new year's regime and goes out for a morning run, and what happens to me? I lose my precious time with Nate.

I pounded the ground with my fist, anger taking over me and then just as quickly, the emotion changed back to heartache and I hung my head and cried.

He had the nerve to interrupt that as well.

"Are you okay?"

Just moments earlier, Nate was here, but now he was gone because of this guy. I stood up tentatively, my legs feeling weak from chasing after him and perhaps the fact that I had skipped breakfast -- again. I steadied myself and was prepared to spew verbal bullets at the stranger, until my eyes met his.

Crystalline blue tinged with green, just like Nate's. I opened my mouth to speak, but only a garbled cry came out. Tears started to stream down my face and I took off running. I got to the highway and didn't stop, prepared to take off toward the connecting trail on the other side, when a car sped across, stopping me in my tracks. As soon as it passed, I continued on even though other cars were in line behind it. Horns blared as I dodged ahead, playing a dangerous game of chicken. But I made it across the highway, and to my dismay, so did he.

I noticed his shadow following me. For a moment I hoped it was Nate's, but a glance over my shoulder indicated it was only the stranger who was either a stalker or someone with growing concern for my erratic behavior. Another person to pity me that I didn't need.

"Hey! Are you okay?" he repeated. I heard his footsteps keeping time just behind me.

I rolled my eyes at him and turned around, back for the original trail. I just wanted to get to my woods again. I would lose this guy, find Nate, and be whole. I continued down the incline that I had just traveled up, reached the highway and didn't stop, not even when I hit the pavement and another horn blared its warning. The car swerved to avoid me, but continued on without stopping. I dropped and rolled back to the highway's shoulder where I came to rest with my head in my hands.

If it had been any later in the morning I may not have been so lucky. Except for the one car, the road was empty once more -- albeit the approach of the stranger, who now bent down to help me up.

"Here," he said offering me his hand.

I looked up at him warily. Although the sun was in my eyes, I could still make out his strong frame. He wasn't as tall as Nate, but his chest and shoulders were broader, giving way to a trim waist and toned abs whose outline were visible through the white Under Armour shirt he wore. I reached toward his hand and he easily pulled me to my feet. Once again, I took in his eyes and was more than a bit freaked out that it was as if I were looking into Nate's. I stared without saying a word, which no doubt gave him even more cause to worry about my mental state.

"So...you got a death wish or something?"

That jarred me out of my reverie. "No, I don't. I was...just out for a run and you interrupted me."

"It didn't look like you were running when I first saw you. You were crying."

"Sometimes I do that when I run."

"Well, next time you decide to go for a run maybe you should avoid the highway. That's some game of chicken you've got going on. You could've killed us both."

The nerve!

"I never asked you to follow me!"

He looked at me, sizing me up. I met his gaze, practically daring him to make another sassy comment. He didn't. Instead, he put his hands up as if to show me that he meant me no harm, and ever so slowly and gently brushed some of the rubble from the pavement away from my cheek.

"Good as new," he said lightly.

"Hmmpf."

"Or...maybe not. You wanna talk about it?"

"What makes you think I have anything that needs saying? And to a stranger at that."

He held out his hand. "Ethan. Now I'm not a stranger."

Again, his clear blue eyes met mine. A tingling sensation went up my spine and traveled over my arms in the same way that I had felt when Nate ran his hands over my arms earlier. It warmed me from the morning air. I shook my head at the man before me. I didn't need to talk. I just ran off.

"Be careful," he yelled after me.

Chapter 16 - Nate

Ella, what were you thinking? I ran my hand through my hair and paced nervously, trying to make sense of her actions.

I wasn't angry at the fact that some guy obviously found her to be hot. I mean, what guy wouldn't? I was upset at how reckless she had become as if she didn't give a damn about her own life...a life that was still worth living. To think that she nearly got hit on the same road that took my life was gutting. I should have stayed longer, but somehow when that guy...Ethan...when he showed up it felt different.

The look on his face when he first saw her...man, I know that look. It's odd that I don't feel jealousy. Maybe it's because of the way she handed him the 'I'm not impressed look' on a plate. Just like the one she gave me when I first tried to chat her up. Classic Ella. And then as if giving him the cold shoulder wasn't enough she has to turn on her heel and run into oncoming traffic?!

I have to talk to her and get her to understand that I'm okay and I want her to be that way as well. I would spend the rest of eternity ensuring her safety and happiness. The problem is that as soon as I see her, I can't help but take her in my arms. I'd even do it now with the dirt and grime clinging to her cheeks. To me, she's still beautiful.

# # #

"Oh my god, Ella, what happened?" Lily's voice rose an octave when Ella walked into the kitchen. Lily and Zach hadn't strayed far from where she left them before going on her hike. Now, remnants of breakfast were laid out before them. It wasn't croissants and pastries from La Conversation, one of Ella's favorites, but from the looks of it, Zach had done the cooking and I would have thoroughly enjoyed being invited for the spread of sausage, eggs and a loaf of fresh bread from the grocery store bakery.

Lily had enjoyed the lazy Sunday with a new book while Clash of Clans held Zach's attention. That was, until Ella walked in with cuts and scrapes on her face and the emerging sign that a shiner was forming on her cheekbone.

"It's nothing. I fell." Ella started to leave the kitchen, but Zach was too fast, standing up in front of her to get a better look at her injuries.

"How do you fall like that? You didn't hurt just one side of you, which is what happens when someone falls. You took a roll."

"What happened?" Lily pressed.

Ella put her hands on her hips and exhaled, staring at both of them. "Well, mom...dad," she said sarcastically, "I was running back to my car, I guess I wasn't paying attention and another car sort of got in my way."

Lily gasped and covered her mouth with her hand.

"It's a good thing that Nate taught you military rolls." Zach filled in for Lily's inability to form words. "You could have been killed."

"Well, that might have been an improvement," Ella said bitterly.

"What do you mean by that?" Lily stepped forward, putting her hands on Ella's shoulders, but Ella only took another step back.

They squared off until Lily changed her tact. "Do you want some breakfast now? You didn't eat before...running."

"No, thanks."

"I could whip you up some eggs?"

"Lily, I said no. Scrambled eggs are not the cure all for a scrambled heart."

"More like a scrambled head," Zach added under his breath. Lily glared at him and elbowed him in the stomach. Yeah, that was all Zach. He meant well, but when it came to tact, he had about as much of it as a flea.

"You know I'm not serious," he threw in for good measure, although I had a feeling he meant what he said. Besides, he was right.

Ella nodded stiffly and as if echoing my thoughts, she repeated the sentiment. "Maybe you're right. Maybe I'm so messed up from Nate's death that I'll never be the same. And you know what? That's okay with me."

Lily eyed her, a worried expression taking over her face.

"You will be okay," Zach said emphatically. "You're strong."

"You don't know anything."

Zach softened his voice. "I know that we all handle loss in different ways, and we learn to go on."

"You're military. You and Nate...two peas in a pod. You learn how to cage your emotions and deal with loss. Fuck, Nate asked me to marry him and what do I do? I didn't answer. But you know what really sucks? He handled it. He didn't yell; he didn't cry or beg or plead. He just gave me the time I needed and what do I do? I piss it all away."

Ella was crying now, shaking out of control. Lily put her arms around her, but she just took a step back, shaking her head. "I'm not worthy of your sympathy. I couldn't give him the love he wanted. Don't give it to me now," she shot back and stepped out of the room.

"Ella...," Zach called out to her. "In a week, I'm shipping out again. Nate would have been with me and you know it kills me that he's gone. But I have to clear my head and do my job. And you...you have to move on too."

For a moment I thought Ella's tough exterior would melt and that she'd see how everyone was trying to help, but maybe that's exactly what was driving her away. She turned on her heel, calling over her shoulder.

"I'm going to take a shower."

If I could, I would hold her now and show her how much she means to me. I'd talk some sense into her and tell her that Zach is absolutely right. That is, right after I had the chance to kiss every one of those cuts and scrapes better.

Chapter 17 - Ella

Damn them for thinking they know what I need. The only thing I need is the peace that I found in the woods. Nate's presence was stronger there and I felt...like I belonged with him. I wonder how much difference it would have made to either of our lives if I had just said yes to him when he first asked me to marry him. What would have changed? Maybe we would be out celebrating with Zach and Lily at a restaurant rather than hiking on that particular Sunday. Maybe we would have chosen to stay in bed on that morning. These thoughts kept me awake...feelings that one moment in time can change everything.

I threw off my hiking boots and peeled off my socks, stepped out of my pants and pulled my shirt over my head. I reached for the shower faucet and as I turned the handle, I felt his hand over mine. I jumped back, but relaxed when I heard his sweet voice whispering in my ear. "Zach and Lily are only trying to help."

I pulled back the shower curtain and smiled a toothy grin.

"You left me," I said, my mood now considerably lighter than my words indicated. I stepped into the shower to join Nate. "One minute we were...you know. And then, that guy had to show up and ruin it."

"He just seemed concerned. We all are," Nate said pointedly.

I ran my hand down the front of his chest, loving the smooth hardness of his body. Matching my movements, he placed his hand just above my breast. "I'm always in your heart."

His words were sentimental, but the feeling of his hand on me produced decidedly more tempting thoughts in me. I placed my hand over his, and pulled his hand downward, encouraging him to touch me. He cupped my breast, letting his thumb gently slide back and forth over my nipple.

"Is this what you would have done to me if that guy hadn't turned up?" I teased.

"And then some..."

"Like?"

Nate bent his head to my breast and ran his tongue over my nipple, flicking back and forth until it was hard. "Like this," he said continuing to kiss my breast.

"And?"

"And like this..." he kept his mouth on my breast, but let his hands roam over my back and then come to rest on my bottom. I pressed into him, feeling his hardness against me. I could feel the tip of him pressing against me and I opened my legs to feel him even closer.

"Uh uh," he said lowering his mouth to my waist and then, going down on bent knee, he lowered it even more to where my hip bone jutted out.

"We haven't made love in so long. Maybe we could...Don't you want me?"

"More than you can imagine, but first..."

He lowered me to the tiled bench seat and then instructed me to open my legs wide. Staring up at Nate's gorgeous body, slick from the water and tanned against the white of the shower, who was I to argue. I did as he wanted and then he guided the shower head to spray between my legs, the pressure of the water making me feel even more turned on.

I closed my eyes and enjoyed the sensation, while Nate reached for the soap, scented with jasmine like the kind that grew on the shoulder of our hiking trail. He got his hands sudsy from the soap and then ran his hands over my arms, gently removing the trace bits of rock that were still stuck to my skin thanks to my scramble with the pavement.

The combination of the warm pressure between my legs, his hands running over my body, my thoughts and sensations were on overload. "Nate, I'm going to..."

"Not yet, you're not," he said knowing me better than I knew myself. He lowered himself in front of me, placing a hand on each of my knees and took his place between my legs. His mouth soon replaced the sensations of the water. He alternated between using his tongue in a gentle flicking motion with his mouth that expertly sucked me.

I grabbed onto his head, pulling him toward me with an urgency that said I didn't want him to stop. Even more, I didn't want him to leave.

My body was prone to give itself fully to the beautiful movements of his mouth, but there was something else that I wanted. I tugged slightly on a bit of his wavy brown hair and then bit my lip mischievously when he looked up at me.

"Yes? Was there something else I could do for you?" he teased.

I scooted forward on the bench in response. He knew what I wanted and he grabbed my bottom and hoisted me up. I pulled my legs around his waist and then as he turned us around and he took the seat that I had occupied, he slowly lowered me onto his magnificent shaft and I sighed with the pleasurable feeling of how he filled me.

Our lovemaking was slow and luxurious. I moved up and down him, guided by his strong arms. There was no need to hurry because I didn't want it to end. The water felt so warm and wonderful. My head was starting to spin from the heat, but I didn't mind. It only added to the erotic sensation and Nate had his hands planted firmly around my hips, holding me safe.

"Why did you leave earlier?" I whispered in his ear as I pressed against him.

"We had company," he said in a lazy whisper. I noted how peaceful and quiet his voice seemed to me.

"So? We could have been doing this. You made me wait for it."

"Some things are worth waiting for."

I took in the double meaning of his words. "Nate? You're talking about me."

He didn't answer. He didn't have to. But then, as if to ease my mind, his hands traveled up my back, gently rubbing tiny circles over my skin. I matched the motion with my hips, feeling myself close to the edge as I moved against him.

"Zach misses you," I said, not really knowing why that thought entered my mind at this particular moment.

"You wanna invite my platoon buddy into the shower? I draw the line there," he said with a smile, his jovial tone bringing me out of the last of my sorrow.

"Nah, Lily wouldn't like that."

I heard her voice calling to me.

"Speaking of Lily..."

"No, don't leave Nate. She can wait. Let me stay here with you for just a bit longer."

Again, Lily's voice sounded outside the door.

"Just a minute," I mumbled, but it must have been drowned out by the sound of the shower because she continued to call my name.

"Let's just finish..." I implored Nate.

But just like before when the other hiker showed up...what was his name...it doesn't matter...whoever he was, he caused Nate to disappear and now it was happening again. In fact, everything seemed slightly out of reach for me right now. Nate was fading, but Lily's voice kept calling my name. And in spite of my persistent, albeit annoyed responses, she kept shouting.

"Sheesh, can't anybody have privacy these days? First the hiker, now Lily," I complained, holding onto Nate as tightly as I could, feeling the water rush over my face. "We're going to have to find some sort of paranormal hotel room or something."

"Hey," he said and placed a hand underneath my chin, tilting my head up so I could stare into those amazing eyes, "I'm always here for you."

There was nothing I wanted more in the world than to be with Nate so why then when I looked back into his eyes did I see those of Ethan staring back at me?

Part II

Chapter 18 - Ethan

"Good morning."

"You? What are you doing here?"

Even in this condition she was beautiful. I wasn't supposed to notice, but I couldn't help it. Her wavy brown hair fanned out over the pillow and although it was straighter than when I had seen her on the mountain, probably from her lying on it for a good two days, it still made her look like an angel.

"First things first. Do you know where you are?"

She looked at me with sudden confusion as if I had indeed woken her up from a dream. I watched as she took in the hospital room and the shock registered on her face. Her skin was already drawn and pale from lack of nutrients, and her eyes looked large and hollow.

"Why am I in a hospital? And what are you doing here?"

"Can I sit down?"

Even in her weakened condition, she had the strength of character to roll her eyes at my request, but then raised her eyebrows and indicated that I could take a seat on the bed.

"Well? Are you a stalker or something?"

"I'm actually one of the doctors here. Meeting you earlier was pure coincidence, although I would have liked to have gone running with you."

"You wouldn't have been able to keep up." Her voice sounded as weak as her body, but her pride was certainly strong.

"Touché. I'm Dr. Feinfield, but since I already introduced myself, please call me Ethan," I said and extended my hand to her as I had when I first saw her on the hiking trail.

"I remember," she said with apparent disinterest. "So, Dr. Ethan...did I twist my ankle or something? Pass out from hitting my head on a rock?"

"Ella...do you mind if I call you by your first name?"

Again she rolled her eyes, but at least she shook her head.

"Great. No, you did not twist your ankle, although it sure seemed like that was your intention the other day. Do you always run trails that are meant for walking?"

"Yes. I do."

"Do you know that your blood sugar was dangerously low when you were admitted? Your iron levels are totally out of whack. You're anemic."

"So when can I go home?"

I ignored her question and asked a real zinger of my own. "Ella, did you try to kill yourself?"

"What? No, of course not. Has anyone ever told you that your bedside manner sucks?"

"I'm working on that." In truth, I had heard it before, but losing someone close had a way of making me build up walls. There was something about Ella, however, that made me want to be better. Maybe it was the haunted look in her eyes when I first saw her or the way she ran...Whatever was bothering her that day, it was obvious that it wasn't a one off.

"What kind of doctor are you anyway? You mention a myriad of ailments, although I have to say, I feel fine." With that, she pulled back the covers, revealing toned legs that didn't escape my gaze, as she tried to get out of bed. But as to be expected, the lack of food in her system caused her to get light-headed and she slumped to the side, nearly falling out of the bed as fast as she tried to escape it.

I caught her before she went over. Her torso rested in my arms lightly and her face looked up into mine. For a moment, neither one of us said anything. Maybe she was too dizzy to speak, but I didn't have such an excuse. I just couldn't take my eyes off her eyes, her lips. And I so wanted to help her...not only for her, but for me as well.

In some ways, she was frail of both body and mind, and yet there was that sharp tongue of hers that would cut to the heart of the matter and was ready to call me out on any misstep. Nobody had challenged me in that way for a long time.

"I'm a psychologist, and I've been assigned to you."

"Not a psychiatrist," she said pointedly. "But you said *doctor.*"

"It's in the works. I may have misspoken."

"In the works?"

I didn't answer her. Given what her sister had told me, she was obviously hurting and deserved someone who could make a difference and help her. Given my own shortcomings and the demons I fought, I wasn't sure that I was the man for the job.

"Well?" she persisted. "What does that mean? Is it like baking a cake? You're nearly cooked?"

"I'm in my residency and like I said, you're one of my assignments."

She opened her mouth to speak, but I suppose she decided to practice some restraint and thought it was better to just close it again. As if less than polite words threatened to spew from her, she held it shut in a tight line until the temptation to tell me off became too strong and she started in again.

"I don't want to be 'an assignment.' Furthermore, whatever landed me here was just...I've been busy, okay? I've had a lot on my mind and I haven't eaten properly. That's all."

"A lot on your mind? Like the accident that nearly killed you and took the life of your boyfriend? I'd say that's something to talk about."

"Who told you?"

"Your sister. She thought it would be a good idea if you...consulted with someone, and she thought my credentials were a good match. And apparently, your employer is insisting on a full psychiatric evaluation and course of treatment before you're allowed to return to work."

Her mouth fell open with the news. I couldn't blame her. It was a lot to take in, but I never expected her reaction to it.

"My job may insist that I see a shrink, but I know they wouldn't pay for it. I also know that my sister can't afford it, which makes me suspect that there's some reason the hospital paired me up with you. What did you do that was so wrong to get you saddled with me?"

Chapter 19 - Ella

The idea of having to see a psychologist is ridiculous. As if this guy has even enough life experience to help me, not that I need any help. Honestly, he doesn't even look old enough to have lived through anything that would give him the empathy and understanding to be a support to me, if that's what I was after.

I studied his face as he sat at the edge of my bed, writing notes as if I were some sort of school project. His hair was dark and wavy with a wayward bit that kept falling in his eyes. He would flip his neck in an irritating way to push it out of the way rather than take time from his writing to use his hand. I guess I must be a fascinating subject to him. He probably doesn't get out much. Hmm, maybe we do have something in common. Besides the hiking, that is.

"Why were you on my hiking trail that day?" I asked breaking the silence. It wasn't like I really wanted to strike up a conversation with him, but it bothered me that he was on my trail -- mine and Nate's. In the years that Nate and I were together we had never seen another person on that trail. It was part of its appeal to us...our private refuge. It's just too weird that I run into Ethan on the trail and then...then this.

"That's my place," he said simply. "I go there most Sundays just before dusk. It helps me clear my head. It's funny, but I never see anyone else there. I guess the terrain is too rough for most hikers."

I nodded my head absently. "I always go in the early morning."

"Yeah, well I decided to go early that day. You mind if I just stay here for a bit?"

"Don't you have some place to go?" I said with an irritation I couldn't hide. A nurse came in to check my I.V., and addressed Ethan briefly.

"Are you requesting sedatives for this patient," she asked as if I wasn't there.

"No, not at this time," Ethan replied and smiled at me as if reassuring me that I wasn't crazy.

The nurse left and he turned to meet my gaze. Again I noticed his eyes and how they were uncannily similar to Nate's. It bothered me and gave me comfort all at once. Maybe they only appeared to be so clear blue because of the blue button down shirt he wore. It was open slightly at the neck, revealing a light dusting of hair on his broad chest. The sleeves were rolled up to his forearms, which were strong and tanned. His hand held his pencil lightly and tapped out a rat-a-tat-tat sound against his pad. It was something that Nate would do, acting boyish even in the most serious of circumstances.

He smiled back at me. "Do you really want me to leave? It's pretty boring here and your discharge orders aren't for one more day."

I sighed loudly. "Fine. So, what are you writing about me?" I asked motioning to his pad.

He turned his pad toward me and revealed his work to me...something I never expected. It wasn't a report at all. Using only a pencil, he managed to create an intricate sketch with varying textures and widths of lines, shadows of light and dark, and the most surprising of all was the subject...me. Only I wasn't lying in an ugly hospital gown with my hair stringy and uncombed. I was in my woods, bending down to pick up a flower.

I stared at the drawing in silence, taken in by how well he recreated the setting of the trail without actually being there to copy it. "It's amazing. How do you recall the details so well?"

"I told you. I go there pretty much every weekend." He looked at his own work. "You didn't comment on the rest of the picture."

I knew he was referring to his drawing of me, but how could I comment? Nate used to sketch me when he was overseas. He said it gave him something to do at night and he could recall every detail of my face. I had never known anyone else who could draw with such detail from memory.

"You have too much time on your hands," I said and turned away, not able to look at the picture for it brought back too many painful memories. I wanted to be there, not just look at it.

"Right again. So, let's start. Something easy? What's your job?"

"Do we really have to do this?"

"Yes," he said simply.

"I'm a research analyst and fact checker for an online news service."

"Sounds interesting."

"It isn't, but I suppose it beats asking strangers about their lives."

He smiled. "You're funny. I can only imagine how clever you must be when you haven't slept for two days."

"You'll never know."

"Never say never," he retorted before delving into his next question. "Hobbies?"

Granted it was another easy question, but I wasn't used to talking about myself, certainly not with someone as handsome as Ethan. It wasn't like I wanted to notice that fact, but damn, it was impossible not to. Besides, lying here in a gown that opened up in the back, no makeup, messed up hair, even more messed up mind, I felt exposed.

"If you want me to answer your questions, then you have to answer mine. Otherwise...no deal."

"You know, you don't have much of a leg to stand on considering I can walk out of here and you can't, but since I think it would be a good idea for us to get to know each other...since we are going to be spending time together..." he said pointedly, "I'll comply."

"That's big of you."

And then, he kicked off his shoes and got comfortable on the foot of my bed. He actually grabbed a spare pillow that had been discarded on a chair, propped it under his chest and lay down.

What was even more shocking was that my heart did a little flip flop when he looked up and smiled at me, not just with his mouth, but those damn blue eyes as well.

Chapter 20 - Ethan

God she was cute...and sassy...and wearing a look that was just so darn sad that I would do anything to wipe it away. And yes, my job did depend on my getting through to her...my tortured past did as well.

"Okay, shoot. What do you want to know?" I said leaning my legs out across the bed.

"You comfy?"

"Very," I smiled.

"When am I getting out of here and why do I need therapy all of a sudden?"

"Tomorrow and because it's not completely clear whether or not you tried to kill yourself."

She stared at me with a look of complete shock. I dropped my smile, hoping to instill in her just how serious this was and with all of my heart, I hoped the look she wore was evidence that she could love herself as much as she had loved her boyfriend.

"I took a couple of pain meds on an empty stomach. That could have landed anyone in the hospital."

"Except not just anyone was experiencing severe depression due to their boyfriend's recent death. Anyway, was that your question because you're using up your time."

"No it wasn't...If I'm such a risk to myself then how did I get assigned to you? You look about twelve."

I smirked. "Cute. I got my bachelor's from U.C.L.A. in biology, transferred to U.S.C.'s Keck School of Medicine, and here I am -- serving my residency. And no, I'm not twelve; I'm 28."

I reached over to the end of the bed where her chart was hanging and picked it up, searching for the piece of information I sought.

"Ahh, here it is...you have no allergies, you're 33, and you like younger men."

She threw her pillow at my head. I guess I deserved it, but something about her made me want to tease her, to coax her out of her melancholy nature.

"Not that young," she said wiggling a finger in my direction.

"But at least I made you smile."

She looked at me without speaking for a moment, as if shocked by the truth...I had made her smile.

"Maybe I'm just amused by the young doctor in residence who likes to lounge around on his patient's beds."

"It's the psychologist in me...that whole lay down on the couch and tell me your troubles thing. I lead by example."

"Oh yeah? Then go ahead, dish."

It was a dare and I was nearly tempted to tell her, to tell her how badly I screwed up while in school and how desperate I was to redeem myself, but I couldn't. It wouldn't be professional and even though knowing something personal about me might make her inclined to open up, I just couldn't go there.

"Let's just say that we all have our...memories. Sometimes, you just need a friend to help you work them out."

"Is that what you think we are? Friends?"

"I'd like to be," I answered her honestly.

"Okay then, friends do things together...like go hiking. So, if you really want to get inside my head, to hear what I have to share, then we do these 'sessions' or whatever you want to call them, on the mountain."

It was totally unconventional and I knew that I could get busted all over again, but hell, it was also the only way I was going to get her to open up to me. Something was seriously bothering her and I wanted...no I needed...to help her. I had lost someone close as well. I knew what she was going through.

"I'm not sure you could keep up with me," I goaded her.

She scoffed. "Are you sure it's not the other way around?"

"How 'bout one or two meetings in my office first -- just so I can make sure you're up for this amazing challenge."

"You're scared of being out run by a girl."

"Maybe," I admitted, and held out my hand for a shake.

She reached out to take my hand and I quickly pulled it back in ultimate coolness -- at least in the coolness of a geeky teenager. "Uh uh...one condition. You get rest; you eat," I said emphatically, "and no more pain meds."

"Okay doc, so how 'bout you bust me outta here?"

Chapter 21 - Ella

Even though I was more than capable of walking, a hospital volunteer -- a senior citizen, no less -- was now charged with pushing me in a wheelchair to the curb where Lily waited for me, hands on her hips. She had visited me twice, each time I asked her to leave. It was either because I was too ashamed for her to see me or too stubborn to admit that I might have the eensiest bit of a problem.

"How are you feeling?" she asked, trying to gauge my mood.

"Fine." A one word answer was about all I could muster at the moment.

She held open the passenger door for me, put my overnight bag in the trunk, and then she turned to thank the woman with white hair who was now able to move at a normal pace thanks to the fact that she lost the baggage that was in her chair.

"Thanks," I called over my shoulder to the volunteer, who had already rolled the chair away and was out of earshot. Lily rolled her eyes at me, letting me know that I may not have to be super nice to family, but I best be civil to others.

I got in the car and closed the door. "I forgot," I said by way of explanation. "She was so quiet; I hardly noticed she was wheeling me -- it felt like we were standing still half the time."

"She probably picked up on that 'don't talk to me, I'm miserable company' vibe you have going."

"Probably," I admitted, which only served to make Lily soften.

"Here," she said handing me a pink pastry box. "It's a surprise."

I hesitated when I saw the label on the box. It was from La Conversation, my favorite place and the one where Nate stopped to get breakfast for us the day he was killed. Lily didn't know, but it was hard to be happy about the reminder. She put the box on my lap and I was shocked by how heavy it was.

"You must have bought out the store!"

"I knew that it was your favorite place, but I didn't know what kind you liked, so...I bought them all. I used to see the empty boxes in your kitchen."

I nodded. "When you would visit on Sundays. Nate and I always took pastries on our hikes."

She grew quiet, realizing what she had done. "I'm sorry, Ella. The last thing you need is a reminder."

"That's not true. Why does everyone want me to forget him? Don't you see, I don't want to forget him!"

Lily had pulled the car out of the hospital parking lot and was now headed slowly through the neighboring streets. I saw her knuckles grip the wheel as if concentrating on her driving was becoming increasingly difficult either due to my shouting or simply the turn the conversation had taken.

I lowered my voice, but continued nonetheless. "I'm sorry for shouting, but you have to stop hovering over me as if...as if...Oh, I don't know what I want to say any more!" I said and pushed my hands through my hair.

"As if you might try to kill yourself? Huh, Ella?"

"I didn't try," I insisted. "If I had wanted to..." I lowered my voice to a mutter, "I'd have been successful."

"What was that? You didn't say what I think you said."

"No. I didn't say anything."

We drove in silence for a couple blocks. The strain between us was horrible. We had always been so close. Even when I met Nate, it was another way that Lily and I bonded. She loved him and when he introduced her to Zach, it was even better. The four of us were inseparable. If she only knew what I knew.

"I need to tell you something," I said, bridging the subject.

Lily put her hand on my leg while she drove. "Ella, I love you. You can tell my anything."

"Even if it's hard to believe?"

"I'm your sister."

Okay then.

"Lily, I can see him. I can talk to him, touch him. He's real."

"Oh Ella." So much for being able to tell her anything. Her face dropped and her voice went silent. She didn't have to go on, I knew exactly what she was thinking. That I was imagining Nate because I was so desperately lost without him. Or worse, that I had completely lost my mind.

"Say it. Go ahead; tell me I've gone to crazy town."

"Well...that is a lot to take in. Would you believe it if you were in my shoes? I just want so badly to help you and I don't know how."

Lily pulled the car over to the curb. She put it in park and reached out her hand and took mine in her own.

"It's true, Lily."

She nodded at me, but tears started to well up in her eyes. She didn't believe me, and how could I blame her?

"Ella, you know that your work has insisted on therapy, and I agree that it's important for your full recovery. I'm not saying that you intended to hurt yourself, but it's not hard to understand how you ended up in the hospital. You weren't eating...sleeping. You took pills. You need to talk to that doctor."

"Ethan," I said dully.

"Is that his name? Maybe he can help. Please, just give him a chance."

Lily said her piece, which served to bring back her composure. She pulled back out into the traffic, but nearly rear-ended the car in front of us when I delivered the real zinger of the conversation.

"I already agreed to speak to him, but only once or twice. Anything beyond that takes place on my mountain."

Chapter 22 - Nate

I could tell that Ella wasn't herself when she got back to the house. I suppose nobody is in top form when they get out of the hospital, but she seemed particularly down. As soon as she entered her room, she lay down on the bed and cried herself to sleep.

"Ella, I want you to be happy," I whispered softly and brushed back a wayward strand of her beautiful, wavy brown hair. I bent my head to kiss her neck. She stirred and rolled into my arms.

"Nate, I'm happy...when you're with me."

"We need to work on you being happy all of the time, or at least, most of it."

She snuggled her head onto my chest and I heard her inhale deeply, filling herself with my scent. I did the same every time I was with her so that I could remember every fiber of her being. I was content just lying next to her, holding her close, but Ella had other ideas.

She rolled onto her side and locked eyes with me. She was so close. I felt the rise and fall of her chest against mine, and noted how our heartbeats matched and beat in unison. My hand ran over her back and then automatically slipped lower to caress her bottom, and that was all the encouragement she needed. She threw her leg over mine so that our hips pressed together.

"I want you, Nate. Now. No more waiting."

With that declaration, she pressed her mouth against mine. I felt her urgency and longing because it was matched by my own. Her hand traveled down my leg and strategically rested right where I needed it most.

In one swift motion, I flipped her onto her back and proceeded to layer kisses from her collarbone to between her breasts, moving slowly along her stomach and then traveling downward to her hips and finally, between her legs.

"Please..." she moaned.

She spread her legs, giving me ample room to continue. I placed my hands underneath her hips and pulled her against my mouth. My tongue moved slowly and when she called out my name, I continued a steady, circular motion that made her grip my hair and arch herself even harder against me, until she sighed...an expression of pure contentment.

"That wasn't fair."

I laughed, knowing immediately what her complaint would be. "It was plenty fair."

"What about you?"

"I'm satisfied in knowing that you're happy."

She stretched out and I pulled her back against me, wrapping my arms around her so she felt safe.

"You'll stay?"

"Until you don't need me." I ran my hands up her arms, ensuring she was warm.

"I'll always need you."

"Ella..." I hesitated, unsure how to bridge the subject that weighed on my mind.

"What is it?" she said, her voice already sleepy.

"Give the new guy a chance."

"What new guy?"

"Ethan."

She blew out a breath of air as if to say 'yeah right'.

"Let him help you."

She didn't reply; she was already fast asleep.

Chapter 23 - Ella

I can imagine so many things I'd rather be doing today than driving across town, wasting an hour in traffic, to talk to Ethan about my depression, which mind you, is totally natural considering my loss.

The traffic along Ventura Boulevard was particularly slow since it was lunch time. I glanced out the window as I passed the French Crepe Company where Nate loved the seafood crepes. I could picture him and his funny way of eating them -- first opening up the crepe, tearing off a piece of the end to taste before it was covered in the creamy sauce, then finding a shrimp, then a scallop, and tasting one tiny piece of each, before he would fold the whole thing back up and eat it the way the chef had intended.

There were too many memories associated with going out, which was why I preferred to just go to work or my mountain. Of course I had memories of Nate on the mountain, but it wasn't painful because he was there with me. Here, I only felt sorrow.

As I pulled into the parking structure next to Encino Hospital, where Ethan had an office, I realized that I had no memories associated with this place beyond Ethan. If work wasn't going to allow me to come in, then this might actually be the next best place for me. I found a parking spot next to the elevators and took it to the ground floor. When the bell dinged and the doors opened, I walked myself and my new and improved attitude toward the hospital lobby.

Chapter 24 - Ethan

I had spent the last fifteen minutes shuffling papers back and forth on my desk, trying to keep myself busy while waiting for our appointment. This felt like some sort of test on so many levels.

My billable hours were down this month, my boss so aptly informed me when I tried to get myself dismissed from this case. There was something that reminded me of my loss every time I spoke with Ella -- something that made me fear not only for her well-being, but my own, if I couldn't help her.

I had been down a similar road before and hit a dead end. While in the height of my internship I lost my girlfriend to suicide. I was studying and working ridiculous hours. There was little time for food and sleep, let alone a relationship, which is what the older students and doctors told us. So when our relationship started to suffer and crumble, I told her that I needed a break. I never saw her again after that night.

I should have recognized the signs. The professional in me knows that there was probably little I could do to help her, but as her former boyfriend, I wonder if I did everything I could have done. All I knew for sure was that I was never going to lose a patient.

But the connection I felt to Ella was dangerous. I felt drawn to her, an unnatural pull that I couldn't explain. It was more than being attracted to a pretty girl or wanting to help a patient. It was both at once and neither and completely doing my head in.

I knew Ella was under psychiatric mandate by her company to be here, so I needed to get her in a functional state and back to work in their minds. I already noted that she didn't want to be here, but was in no shape to continue on her own.

She didn't want to be here. I wasn't sure I wanted her here. And yet, we were bound to work together to vanquish whatever troubles burdened each of our minds. I didn't want to be her doctor; I wanted to date her. I couldn't dare date her because she needed help. She was hurting and vulnerable and I had a chance to right a wrong. I had a chance to heal both of us.

I moved the papers from one side of the desk to the other, then back again trying   to   make   it look...right...professional...capable. I didn't need her knowing that I had just spent the last hour waiting for the chance to talk to her again. What worried me most was not that I had to consult with her, but just how much I wanted to.

The light on the wall suddenly glowed, telling me that a patient had pressed it on the other side of the door. I jumped out from around my desk, and opened the door leading to the waiting room.

"Hi," I said a bit more eagerly than I had intended.

Her tone was much more reserved, shy even. "Hi."

"Do you want to come in?"

Her eyebrows went up and she gave me a look that said 'as if I have a choice and have you ever done this before' all crossed in one.

"I meant...why don't you come in and we'll get started."

She crossed the room without saying a word, first approaching the couch and then thinking better of it, and taking a seat in front of my desk.

"You don't want to sit over there and be more comfortable?"

She looked at the couch and aptly answered, "I think I would be more comfortable in the uncomfortable chair."

I gave her a tight-lipped smile, knowing exactly what she meant. I really had no idea how to start. I knew she didn't want to talk about the incident that landed her in the hospital and bringing it up would only serve to build up a wall between us. After another awkward moment of silence, I decided the best thing to do would be the unexpected.

I reached for a writing pad and heard her sigh.

"Here we go," she said.

"Here we go and what?" I asked.

"You're reaching for the pad. That means you're going to take notes on me like I'm some sort of zoo animal." She watched me writing something on the pad, holding it close so she couldn't see.

Finally, I revealed what I had done.

"Another drawing? Why?" she asked, but came around to where I sat.

She leaned over my shoulder and I immediately smelled her perfume, a light scent of jasmine like the kind that blooms at night. A tendril of her long, wavy hair brushed forward and tickled the side of my face. Without thinking, I reached for it and held it between my fingers.

"Oh sorry," she said and straightened up.

God, I'm like some sort of weird hair toucher. It was just so...there. And it smelled so good.

I handed her my writing pad that featured a picture of a house surrounded by trees. "Your turn."

"I can't draw. Certainly not like this."

"Go on. Add something to it. A bird in the tree, a cat sitting on the front steps, anything."

"Is this part of my therapy?"

"Let's just call it part of getting to know each other."

She took the pad and crossed back to her chair, taking a bit of the wind out of my sails as she moved farther away. As she drew, she bit her lower lip and I gazed at their rosy red color, unable to tear my eyes away.

Finally, she turned the pad toward me. She had added a swing to the wrap-around porch that I had sketched. "That's not bad," I said, unable to suppress the surprise in my voice. "I thought you would totally suck, but this..." I said tapping a pencil to the picture, "pretty good."

"Gee, thanks," she said and laughed. "Are you always this complimentary with potential suicide patients?"

I took the bait and the opening. "Is that how I should classify you? Did you do it?"

She met my gaze and held it. There was warmth in her eyes. She smiled and shook her head. "The truth?"

"Yeah, give it to me. I'm a trained professional. I can handle it."

Again she laughed and the sound was lyrical. It filled me with happiness. I wanted to make sure she laughed everyday.

"I'm not the happiest person right now, but I'm not crazy enough to hurt myself."

I nodded. She was like a cat that I didn't want to scare off. Gentle, but with claws. I had made a start and there was no need to push it.

I picked up the pad again. After drawing a few lines, I turned it toward her.

"Hangman? Really?"

"It's a really hard word. You'll never get it."

"I like a challenge," she whispered while she took the pad and counted the letters.

"So do I," I said, smiling back at her.

Chapter 25 - Ella

Weird. That's the word that comes to mind when I contemplate why in the world my mind keeps straying toward thoughts of Ethan. Just stop it! I tell myself as I drive to work.

The traffic was heavier than usual, but it didn't serve to irritate me or create any anxiousness. Nobody at work would bat an eye if I walked in late. The way everyone tiptoed around me, even Lily, was making me crazy -- or crazier they would say. Ethan was the only one who treated me normally, teased me even.

I smiled to myself remembering our game of hangman.

"There has to be a vowel. You're obviously cheating," I called him on the impossible word. I paced in front of his desk for a minute while he smiled at me, wearing a smug look as if he had already won.

"Don't look so pleased with yourself. I just need to think for a minute. May I?" I said indicating the couch.

"Be my guest."

"Come sit here with me. Otherwise it just looks like you're at the big grown-up desk and I'm the messed up one on the couch."

I sat down in the middle cushion with my legs criss-cross applesauce and he sat next to me, pad in hand.

And then, I got him. "Y."

"Why? Why do I like spending time with you?" he teased.

"You know which 'Y' but...is that true?"

He added the letter to the third dash he had drawn. "You surprise me, and yes, it's true."

I raised my eyebrows and pointed to the paper. "Give me that," I said, indicating his pen.

R-H-Y-T-H-M. I wrote it without hesitation.

He crumpled up the piece of paper into a tight wad and threw it at me playfully. "Ella, you are one mean hangman player."

"That I am," I said, lobbing the paper back at him. And that's when I really took notice of him. He had his arms tucked behind his head as he leaned back on the couch, totally at ease. He was so easy to talk to. Either he was damn good at his job, or he was just that type of guy...the type you wanted to confide in because he would make everything better.

He wasn't pretentiously dressed in a jacket, just his white button down, rolled up at the cuffs, and unbuttoned once at the neck. His forearms were tanned and strong, his Adam's apple protruded as he laid his head back looking up at his own ceiling, lost in thought. But he must have read mine for suddenly the silence felt a lot heavier as he moved his hands onto his knees and met my gaze straight on.

Neither one of us broke the stare. Our bodies sat close to each other on that couch, but now that he was looking at me, I was very aware of how close my head was to his as my eyes suddenly wandered to his lips. Why was I staring at his lips? It's not like I wanted to be kissed, and yet, I couldn't help wondering what it would feel like. I swallowed hard. He slowly leaned into me, so carefully as if afraid that I would bolt, and part of me wanted to, but the other part -- the stronger part, or maybe the dumber part -- just stayed put.

We leaned in closer to each other, moving in sync. My eyes stayed on his lips and his on mine. We didn't dare make eye contact for fear that the other would say something to end the moment. His hand was still planted firmly on his own knee, but then he slowly moved it toward my face and brushed the hair out of my eyes. A few strands remained between his fingers as if he wanted to keep a connection between us because then he had to go and ruin it.

"Ella, you are so beautiful, inside and out."

"But..." I whispered, knowing it was coming.

"There is no but. There's just me and I'm here to keep you safe and...nothing more."

Safe. It was the same word that Nate had spoken to me. I nodded, feeling both happy in the knowledge that I had a friend, confidante, whatever he was to me, but also feeling rejected at the same time. And then, with that feeling came guilt. Crazy guilt that I had somehow contemplated cheating on Nate and it tore me up inside.

As his hand continued its hold on a stand of my hair, soothingly running itself through a small section in a relaxed rhythm, I felt that he was struggling with whatever didn't happen as well.

I looked up and met that beautiful gaze, the same one Nate wore, and leaned into him burying my head against his chest. His arms didn't hesitate to wrap around me. The moment had changed. He held me protectively, not with any lust, and it was just what I needed.

Ethan spoke softly while still holding me. "Maybe you're right, Ella. This is more than nice, but maybe we shouldn't be so...alone. You wanted to go for a hike. I think the great outdoors is a great idea."

Did he just say *more than nice*? So I wasn't imagining it and he felt it too...whatever *it* was. He felt so strong and safe, like something I hadn't felt since Nate... And yet, I needed distance. I sat up straight and scooted a few more inches over even though I was highly aware that I didn't really want to move away from him and at the same time, I wanted to bolt from the office. My heart was pounding from nerves, anxiety and even the rush of being so close to him. I needed to get away to the one place where I always felt...right.

"My mountain?"

"Let's try it."

Chapter 26 - Ethan

I slowed down the car on a dangerous stretch of Mulholland Highway. If anyone came barreling up behind me, they would certainly plow right into my bumper, not expecting someone to be stopped here. This wasn't where I normally stopped on my hikes. When we met accidentally it must have been on the return loop for me while she was just starting out. If I had been just five minutes later on that day, I would never have run into her. Fate is a fickle friend.

I jogged down the highway to where she indicated her trail head started. Finally, I spotted the marker. It was barely visible from the road, but as Ella indicated, it was exactly 4.1 miles after a bend with a large oak tree opposite. Remind me never to get directions from that girl again. The experience was a scavenger hunt all its own.

There weren't any other cars parked on the narrow expanse of shoulder and the sinking feeling that I may have been stood up hit me. I got out of the car and paced back and forth, craning my neck downward to see just how rough this part of the trail could be.

"Don't be so pathetic." I chided myself aloud for being disappointed at the possibility that she wouldn't show up.

I told myself that it wouldn't be so bad if she was a no-show. We'd just go back to meeting in my office...the way it's supposed to be. I kicked at a bit of the dirt, thinking that would certainly be more appropriate, but perhaps not so conducive for getting her to open up. A car rounded the bend and I looked up anxiously only to see it continue on. Get a grip. I looked at my watch and decided to give her five more minutes. Ten tops. And then my mind went straight back to our last session. On the plus side, it was productive. We connected. On the negative side...we really connected. I held her and she just fit. Her eyes looked at me with total trust and her mouth was so...kissable.

I paced back and forth waiting. This was not good, but I could change it. "It's important to keep lines of communication open," I reasoned to a bird that landed a few feet from me. It flew off, probably recognizing that it was in close proximity to a crazy person.

Still no sign of her. At least I wouldn't make an ass out of myself by not being able to keep up. I innately knew that she would be a strong runner. My reasoning probably had something to do with the fact that I had glimpsed her gorgeous legs, shapely and fit, on more than one occasion.

"You're just a pair of ears. That's what she needs." A squirrel dashed off at the sound of my voice.

In truth, I wasn't even supposed to be a friend, although I knew that was what she needed most. My professional training and my instinct were strangely competing with one another. Professional opinion told me that friendship could turn into more and what I could never become was a boyfriend to her. And yet, the other day in my office it felt strangely close to that.

"Just remember why you're here." There was something about the fact that we were doing something together -- other than delving into her problems -- that brought a warmth to my heart because I knew she would be happy here. "And maybe I'll stop talking to myself...along with thinking how nice it was to sit next to her on the couch." That last part I muttered to myself.

Even though she was suffering, she still had a feistiness and a wry sense of humor that I didn't encounter often. Talking to her had been the highlight of my work day while she was in the hospital and I wanted to know her better, not only to help her, but because she was funny and smart and had the most beautiful face.

"Just get a grip. She'll be here."

And then as if some unseen force had willed it to happen, she pulled her red Mini Cooper next to my Range Rover.

"Were you just talking to yourself?" she asked, stepping from the car.

She was wearing jean cut-off shorts, a tank under a surfer's hoodie and hiking boots. Her lean legs stretched on forever and I had to turn my head away to stop from gaping at the sheer beauty of her.

"Of course not," I lied. "It's just a bit chilly this morning so I was..."

"Talking to yourself to keep warm?" she laughed.

"Alright, maybe." We paused to size each other up. She emitted pure confidence and I was scared to death. It should have been the other way around, but out here it would be harder to define the lines of doctor and patient, which was exactly what she wanted. And maybe that wasn't so wrong...being a friend to her first and a doctor second.

"So, glad you found my mountain."

She laughed that wonderful laugh of hers, the one I didn't get to hear often enough. "You mean *my* mountain. You think you can handle running it?"

"Psshhaw...piece of cake," I said with a wave of my hand.

She sized me up for a minute. "You do much trail running?"

"I've been on this trail. And I know how to run. How hard can it be?"

Then she did the most amazing thing. Ever. She looked off into the distance, focusing on something with intense concentration. Like a ballerina, she lifted her right leg behind her, slowly extending her left arm in front of her at the same time. The higher she lifted her leg, the lower her body extended forward with her arm straight out in front, like a weight that maintained the delicate balance until her body, arm, and leg were all parallel with the ground. Her neck stretched long, keeping her head slightly above the line of her body, her eyes remaining fixed. She held the pose for what seemed an impossibly long time before ever so slowly and gently she moved into an upright position once more, lowering her arm and leg and staring at me as if to say, "Well, sucker...try that."

"Wow."

She laughed. "Trail running is more than running and hiking. It's all about balance and concentration." She raised her eyebrows once. "You're sure about this?"

Feeling even more out of my comfort zone, I answered truthfully. "You didn't give me much choice."

"That I didn't," she admitted.

"What about this place makes you happy?" I might as well start the ground work toward her recovery and I wanted to know what it was about this place that brought her back.

But she hesitated. Her breathing hitched as if I had inadvertently stumbled upon the very thing that needed to be discussed.

"I think we should postpone the talking and get to the running."

Yep. I had found...something. But I wasn't going to push. She needed a friend, an ear, my psychological expertise...and as she looked at me and our eyes met again, I tried to push any inappropriate thoughts out of my mind, but I couldn't. I wanted to hold her and tell her it would be okay again one day.

Instead, I smiled and said, "Lead the way."

Ella smiled and I knew then and there, this was the right decision. There was an easiness about her here that I didn't see when she was cooped up in the hospital or in my office. This is where she felt alive. If she wasn't my patient, I could fall for a girl like her.

She bent over to pick up a wildflower and tuck it behind her ear. I did the same.

"What are you doing?" she stared at me, laughing at how ridiculous I must look with a daisy poking out of my hair.

"What? You've got one," I said turning my head and jutting my chin into the air like a model would to better show off the flower.

"Oh, so you want to play follow the leader? You're on," and she took off at a run.

"Ella, wait..." I shouted, but it was too little too late. "Shit..." I said under my breath, took a deep breath and took off after her.

Chapter 27 - Ella

I have no idea why I wanted to bring him here...to my place...mine and Nate's. But for whatever reason, I felt compelled to share it with him. Ever since Nate's death, I haven't felt happy except for the times when he visits me, and except for the moments I spend with Ethan.

But, I couldn't help but notice that the more time I spent with Ethan, it felt as if my connection to Nate was waning. I know it's selfish, but I want to feel the connection to both of them. I needed to know that Nate would be okay with this, and just maybe, I'll find the answers here.

I could tell that Ethan was interested, but he was decent. The way he looked away when our eyes met. I smiled remembering the look we shared in his office. It sent my stomach into a backflip and it had been a very long time indeed since I felt like that. It propelled me forward, making me take to the trails in the manner that I had trained with Nate. Running faster and harder, instinctively knowing how to land on the dips of the narrow pathway, when to push harder as the grade turned into a steep incline, and when to jump and leap over sections that threatened to turn over my ankle as it once again became a steep downward descent.

The woods where Nate and I would stop and eat were probably just another two miles ahead. I knew I should slow down and wait for Ethan to catch up, but the wind rushing around my face set me free and felt so good. It cleared my head and made me see life a bit clearer. Clear enough to know that Ethan had something in his past that troubled him. There was some demon tugging on his heart strings as well. It wasn't just the doctor-patient thing that kept him at arm's distance.

I shook my head and jumped down from my current path to another ledge below, avoiding the sharp rocks that jutted up and the poison oak that stretched into the present path. I placed my hands on my knees, bending over to catch my breath. When I stood back up, I took note of the beauty of the day. It was a perfect winter morning with the sun shining, but a chill in the air. So peaceful and quiet.

I sat down on a rock and lifted my face toward the sun, letting it warm my face and I waited for Ethan to catch up. Closing my eyes, it felt as if that wondrous warmth was a soft embrace, wrapping around my back, and that's when I realized it was Nate...

His breath tickled my neck as he held me from behind.

"Where have you been?"

"I've missed you too," he replied and turned me around to face him.

My mouth found his immediately and the feel of his arms pulling me into his embrace felt even warmer than the morning sun. It felt like home. He gently stroked my back and I rested my head on his shoulder.

"Oh Ella...you deserve every happiness," he said stroking my hair.

"I'm happy...now." I looked up and our mouths met again. This time I parted my lips, his tongue gently weaving its way around mine, making a tingle travel up my legs and stomach. I ran my fingers through his hair and he held me even closer.

"I need to feel you," I said in a husky voice and leaped onto his lap, facing him and wrapping my legs around his waist. I pressed against him and immediately felt him harden against me.

"We haven't done this here...since..." he started.

"No, don't talk about that day," I said silencing him with my mouth. We kissed more, our impulses taking over. I threw my head back, giving him easy access to my neck, where I loved being kissed by him. Nate didn't hesitate to oblige my desires. His mouth went to my neck and layered kisses along it, lowering his mouth to my collarbone and then when his hand went to my breast...

"More," I begged.

He lifted my hoodie above my head and tossed it behind me. For a moment, I worried about it landing in the poison oak, but the gentle movement of his hands caressing my breasts quickly erased all other thoughts from my mind.

"E-L-L-A..." It was one of my favorite bedroom games that Nate had so graciously extended to the woods today. He traced each letter of my name with his tongue, running it over my nipple, and then doing the same with his finger, gently starting with the first letter and continuing to the last, until I couldn't stand the sweet torture and we moved onto something even more erotic.

But this time, he looked up and cocked his head as if hearing something in the distance.

"Don't stop."

"We have to...we'll have to continue this another time."

I wrapped my arms around his neck and rested my head against him as I had before, but this time, it felt like a different sort of deja vu. I was instantly reminded of how it had felt when Ethan held me on his couch.

"Nate, you know I'll always love you."

"I know that," he said, once again, running his hand through my hair. "Please Ella, I need you to understand something...my happiness...it's totally wrapped up in your peace...your happiness."

"What are you saying?"

And that's when I heard footsteps, coming fast and loud over the grade. Ethan.

The place where Nate and I had stopped was on a ledge just below the path where Ethan was running, he would never see me unless I called out. I could never imagine that I would feel conflicted like this, except I did. I was torn between them. I wanted to call out so Ethan didn't take a wrong turn, and yet, I didn't want Nate to leave.

But Nate made the choice for me. He was gone.

"Ethan! There's poison oak," I shouted out, which ended up being a mistake since my voice came out of nowhere, taking him by surprise and causing him to misjudge the drop that occurred just before where I was resting.

He went down hard, his footing stumbling in the dry dirt that caused him to slide over the embankment to the next ledge down. He stumbled and went head over foot, grazing his leg against tumbleweed and stones as he went.

"Shit," we both exclaimed at the same time although the expletive erupted from him due to the undoubted pain he was experiencing and from me at seeing him take a nasty fall until he landed just above me.

I grabbed onto a few plants that unlike the ones that had affected Ethan, were not dried out with thorns or of the variety that would inflict skin rashes, and used them to pull myself up to where he still sat sizing up his leg that was bleeding from a nasty gash.

"Let me take a look," I offered.

"Do you have a first aid kit on you?"

"No."

"You run like a bat outta hell and you don't bother to bring a first aid kit?"

"I've never needed one," I said pointedly. "You shouldn't run like that on this incline," I said indicating the trail that took him out.

"Firstly, you were running like that and second, you called my name. I turned to look for you."

I gave him a sheepish look. "Sorry."

He wiped a bit more blood away from his leg. "I'll live. Anyway, what were you doing down here, off the beaten trail," he joked.

I looked down the ledge into the distance toward the woods, wondering when I would see Nate again and trying to figure out what to say. It wasn't like I could just come out with it. "Oh, nothing much...just getting hot and heavy with Nate while you were nice enough to come here with me." No that wouldn't work. I didn't know why, but just as I felt somewhat guilty for admitting to myself that Ethan was cute, now I felt wrong for being with Nate while Ethan was with me. It was weird and confusing and made no sense. Then again, I should just get used to it because my messed up feelings rarely made sense these days.

"No answer for me?" he prodded again.

I just shook my head. "Thinking," I said simply.

He stood up and reached behind me for my hoodie and shook out a bit of dried leaves that clung to it. "You've got goose bumps on your arms," he noted.

I hadn't felt the cold moments ago when Nate held me, but now a chill enveloped me. Ethan held open the neck of my hoodie and positioned it above my head. In a heartbeat, he had it over my head and was pulling it down over me. I extended my arms through the sleeves that he held apart and when I was once again dressed, he ran his hands over my arms, bringing warmth back to me.

"That's better. You're like a warm-blooded woodland creature now."

I could only nod. Words wouldn't form. It was exactly what Nate had said and done on the day he died.

I stared at him, my mouth hanging open. And then, the tears came without any warning.

"Hey..." he said and without hesitation or any concern about what constitutes 'appropriate doctor-patience distance,' he brought me into his chest and just as I had before, I rested my head against him, listening to his heartbeat if only to know that he was real. My sobs continued and he brought his hand under my chin and lifted my face upwards. He searched my eyes.

"Talk to me," he said in a quiet voice that was both gentle and authoritative all the same. It was the way that Nate used to talk to his men. I had heard Zach say that about him numerous times, not to mention that people at the funeral had said the same.

I had to know. There were just too many similarities. I held his glance as he waited for me to say something. I tried to speak, but I was lost in his eyes. I waited to see if that moment would hit again. The one that said nothing will do, except a kiss.

I bit my lower lip while staring at his mouth, then let my eyes go back to meet his gaze once more. It was an invitation if there ever was one and although he held my gaze, unmoving and without saying anything, I saw him swallow hard and the gears in his head were definitely turning with the possibilities.

"Oh Ella," he said as if it pained him. Then he just pulled me in closer, and held me against him. He was a good man. Perhaps too good, just like Nate.

Chapter 28 - Ethan

God, I wanted to kiss her. How do I repeatedly get myself into this situation? That's a line I can't cross if I'm going to remain unbiased and actually help her. And she needs my help, right now. I know something happened while she was running, but what? The expression on her face tells me that something is troubling her.

I played the moment back in my head over and over as we decided to walk for a bit. She was looking into the distance as if the answer to my question would come to her in a vision.

What had she been doing? She looked dazed, and for a totally inexplicable reason I felt that I had somehow interrupted her. These feelings I had for her were striking me hard and fast, like waves hitting the shore, one after the next. Only with Ella, each wave was more powerful than its predecessor. First, the feeling that I had caught her doing something and then that damn moment that kept passing between us. The one that shouted 'kiss her' you fool!

Even crazier, it felt like I was meant to kiss her. But that was just my subconscious wanting to feel again, which was something that I couldn't let happen.

Her touch interrupted my thoughts as she placed her hand lightly on my shoulder and pulled me back, telling me to stop. "You're hurt," she said indicating my leg. "Sit down for a minute."

"It's nothing. Really." I could not sit down here with her. The attraction was too strong -- my will too weak.

"Ethan, you're really bleeding, and there's a nasty rash forming around it. You probably came into contact with poison oak. This'll help," she said, bending down to pick a few mulberry leaves.

If my leg hadn't felt like it was on fire, I would have carried on. Not that it mattered. Stubborn as she was, Ella just bent down and placed a gentle hand on my calf. Just the slightest touch from her rendered me useless.

"Come on," she said looking up at me. "Don't be a baby."

"How am I being a baby by saying it's nothing?" I said sitting down on a patch of grass next to her.

"Because you're only saying that so I won't play nurse."

"With you Ella, I'd rather play doctor."

Shit. That just came out. And then she gave me the look.

It was a look that said she wasn't totally opposed to the idea.

Chapter 29 - Ella

Okay, I know it was a joke, but then again, it did come out of his head and that means he was thinking it. So, I wasn't alone in my thoughts.

I kept my hand on his leg, but turned my eyes from dressing his wound to checking out his expression. He swallowed hard when his eyes met mine.

"I'm sorry. That came out wrong."

"So, you don't find me attractive?" I pushed.

"I didn't say that."

"And you did say that playing doctor would be fun?"

He swallowed again, and seemed to consider how to avoid answering me. Yet, his eyes told an entire story. He watched me...every bit of me, and I didn't mind. His eyes stared at my mouth and then traveled up to my eyes where they remained.

My hand still remained on his leg, holding the mulberry leaves against him. The distance between us couldn't have been more than a foot and suddenly, I was well aware of his breathing as he waited. It seemed as if he was waiting for me to change the conversation, but that wasn't going to happen.

"Attraction?" I repeated.

"Actually, I didn't specify an adjective. I just said..."

"I know what you said. It wasn't entirely a joke, was it?" I was nervous at being so bold. My tongue inadvertently licked across my lips. He caught that move with his eyes and furrowed his brow as if it troubled him...tempted him. His eyes moved down to my hand that rested on his leg. The one that I still hadn't moved.

"Ella..."

I pressed the fingers of my other hand against his mouth, willing him not to say anything to take it back. And while I sat there, just inches away from him with my fingers lightly resting on his lips, he closed his eyes and his lips kissed my fingers. Again, I noticed the slight frown he wore as if whatever was developing between us pained him.

When he opened his eyes a moment later, I moved my fingers to his jawline and traced along it slowly. Words still didn't escape our mouths, but our eyes spoke volumes.

We both had our reasons to get up and leave, and we both had equal reason to stay. Deciding which emotion would win over seemed to overtake him as he leaned forward, ever so slowly, and placed his hand behind my head, pulling me in for the sweetest, softest kiss I've ever had. He closed his mouth over mine with such tenderness as if worried that either one of us would scare from the moment, but neither one of us did.

He smelled like earth and musk. My senses were swimming with being in his arms. They say that smell is actually the most powerful of our senses, with memories being deeply tied to it. I inhaled his scent and although I wanted to stay in the moment and be with Ethan to try and move on from Nate, I couldn't. He smelled like Nate, so sexy and safe.

My hands traveled to his chest, taking in the strong muscles of his torso. It felt so safe being there in his arms. For the first time in months, my mind was tormented. But then I felt something under his shirt. Dog tags. Just like Nate's. His hand was on the small of my back, slowly moving in small circles...just like Nate would do. He had pulled me onto his lap so my legs wrapped around him and I faced him just as I had done so many times before...with Nate.

It was all too familiar. I opened my eyes and he met my stare.

"Are you alright?" he asked, now holding my hand as if worried I would take off running again at any moment.

There was something different about his gaze and voice. I had noticed how similar his eyes were to Nate's, but now his voice had grown quiet, but still had command, just like Nate's.

I couldn't say anything that wouldn't sound like I had gone completely looney and since he was my shrink, it seemed wisest to just stay quiet. I only shook my head, which he took as my wanting to stop whatever had started between us.

He nodded his head sadly, but held onto my hand for one more moment before moving me off his lap and getting to his feet. He held his hand out for me and helped me up. For a minute we just stood there awkwardly, until he pulled me in for a hug, but it was more of a bear hug than one with seductive intention. Still, it felt reassuring.

"So, you're not going to throw me into the ravine?"

"Why would I do that?" his blue eyes sparkled.

"Because I attacked you like a crazy person."

"One could argue that you're describing me."

I smiled, but couldn't resist the dig that was forming in my mind. "The attacking part...or the crazy part."

"Both."

"Maybe what just happened is like being on a hike....we just took a little detour and now we're back on the trail."

He took my hand firmly in his own and tucked it into his jacket pocket. It was another thing that Nate would do and I caught my breath when he did it. The similarities were coming fast and I had to wrap my head around the craziness that was floating around it.

We walked in a comfortable silence for a minute, my hand still securely wrapped within his, but as I turned to glance at him, every once in awhile his other hand would absently go to the chain he wore around his neck. The dog tags had traveled behind his neck during our "detour" and he fiddled with it to return it to its proper place, before quickly tucking it back into his shirt. It made a soft clinking noise that again reminded me of being with Nate as he would roll over in bed and the sound would remind me that he was near. I used to remember that sound when he was on a mission and pray it meant that he was safe. I had told Nate that when the clasp travels to the front, it's time to put it back behind, and when you do, you're supposed to make a wish. One time when I asked Nate what he wished for, he pretended to complain that it wouldn't come true if he revealed it, but then he naturally admitted the truth -- that he always wished for our mutual safety.

I had to know what Ethan was thinking at that exact moment.

"Did you make a wish?"

"What?"

"Your chain. I saw you flip it to the back. Who's tags are those by the way?"

"My grandfather's. And no, I didn't make a wish, but I will from now on...I'll wish that you are always safe."

My heart pounded a little faster. The realization that Nate's appearances had grown more infrequent as my time with Ethan increased wasn't lost on me. I missed Nate...except when I had Ethan. It was the only time that I felt whole again, but was it enough for me to give up those precious moments when Nate still visited me?

"Let's play a game," I suggested.

"Okay...what is this game?"

"The Lightning Round. Answer my questions in one word."

I had stopped walking. I wanted to see his face, gaze in those familiar eyes and gauge his reaction. I pulled Ethan down to a patch of grass and sat across from him but near enough to hold his hands.

"If you were to build your own house, where would it be? Beach or mountains?"

"Mountains," he said and then motioned his hand around us. "You obviously like it."

"You'd do that for me?"

He nodded once, slowly, and stroked the side of my cheek. "I'd do that."

"Favorite type of takeout," I continued.

"Chinese."

"Favorite Chinese dish."

"Potstickers. Veggie."

I chided him, "One word. Stick to the rules."

"You're a tough cookie."

Memories of Nate teasing me with the same line flooded back into my mind. I sat up on my knees, feeling anxious with the possibility that presented itself.

"Favorite book?"

"Birdsong. Sebastian Faulks."

He leaned closer to me, even though he said he was going to keep his distance. It was as if we had to be close. Something pulling us toward each other and he grew bolder, tossing medical ethics into the wind. His mouth lightly touched my cheek, so softly in fact that it was nearly imperceptible, and then he layered gentle kisses down my cheek, along my jaw and back up my neck until he reached my ear. There, he whispered my name.

"Yes?" I responded, my own voice not more than a mere whisper itself. My lungs barely daring to breathe in his scent again.

"Tell me yours."

"The Lucky One. Nicholas Sparks."

His mouth was still grazing my cheek. I turned so that we were nose to nose, staring into each other's eyes.

"Why that book?"

"It gives me hope. Besides, then I can have a favorite book and movie rolled into one."

He laughed at that and the mood was broken. We straightened up, remembering our vow that I now felt more than ever needed to be forgotten. I was probably insane, but all signs pointed to Ethan being sent to me by Nate. Every glance was similar. They shared every answer. I continued, needing proof of my theory.

"What about you? Favorite movie?"

"Hot Fuzz."

I stared, my mouth having fallen open. Ethan took that for confusion on my part, probably thinking I had never heard of the little English film, but that wasn't the case. Not even close.

"You've probably never heard of it. It's about..."

"Bumbling English cops trying to solve a murder in a sleepy village."

"Exactly Sherlock. You liked it?" he asked hopefully.

"Hated it."

One final question...it would be the clincher in this whole crazy day.

"You've got no cell phone, no book, no nothing...but you've got a beautiful day. How would you spend it?"

"One word?"

"For this one you can have a whole sentence."

"In that case...I'd do this..."

He lay down on his back on a bit of grass that we had claimed as our own, and patted the space next to him. When I laid down next to him, we both stared up at the blue sky. He pointed to a puffy cloud, white as a marshmallow. "I'd watch the shadow of the wind as it moves across the sky, turning clouds into pictures."

Everything was the same. They were the same.

I sat up and picked up a stick to doodle lines in the loose dirty next to where we sat. I doodled circles and lines and then I wrote their names just like a lovesick teen.

N-A-T-E

E-T-H-A-N

Not quite a palindrome, but similar enough to give me another set of chills.

Chapter 30 - Ethan

There are so many things about Ella that haunt me. I look at her and I see my past as well as my future. But I just can't go down that path again. I was told to forgive myself for what happened. I was wrapped up in my own busy life and I wasn't expected to know the signs of a troubled mind, but I do now.

I know that Ella needs me, but not in this way.

Something about her near me makes it impossible not to take her in my arms and what I want to do when she's there is...but that would be a mistake. She's a patient. I'm on dangerous ground and I can feel myself slipping. Hell, I already have slipped, stumbled and fallen. Especially when she looks at me the way she is now, as if she can see right into my soul and she's meant to be there.

Suddenly and for no explicable reason, she moves closer to me and then, without any hesitation she puts her arms around my neck. Her mouth is just inches from mine and I can smell the strawberry scent of her lip gloss.

"I'm supposed to look after you..." I say barely above a whisper. My voice has suddenly caught in my throat because I can't think of anything but kissing her.

"I can't think of a better way than this."

My eyes meet hers before she leaves my gaze and glances at my mouth. It's just a split second before her eyes come back to mine, but it's enough. The idea is once again lodged in my brain and my mouth covers hers. It's not tentative this time. My tongue seeks out hers; my hand wraps around her waist and pulls her in tight.

She moans softly against me and the sound fuels a desire within me, one I'm frightened that I won't be able to stop. If we were somewhere more comfortable and not in the middle of the wilderness, things might be different. But here, I was able to get a hold of my senses. I pull my mouth away, but I leave my hands on her hips. It feels as if I'm struggling to decide whether to pull her in closer again or keep her at arm's distance.

"Ella, I've never done something like this. It's...it's unprofessional and the last thing I want is for you to get hurt."

"But this is beautiful."

Her voice is so innocent and endearing I just want to hold her against me forever. Until, she says something that makes me realize I just can't.

Chapter 31 - Ella

When my family insisted that I see Ethan professionally, they thought I was losing my mind. I knew that I could see Nate. It never once seemed unreal or crazy. But, I could understand how others might find it to be grounds for landing me a seat on the crazy train. This...this was something altogether different. Even I would have trouble believing...If I weren't experiencing the signs first-hand. Nate wanted me to find Ethan...maybe Nate had even become Ethan.

The dog tags, his habits, likes and dislikes...and then there are his moods, his emotions and the way he kisses me. And I can't ignore those eyes...looking at Ethan is a mirror image of staring into Nate's eyes and they melt me every time I gaze within them.

"I know this is going to sound weird, but Nate would want me to be with you." He pulls me into his broad chest and I relish the feeling of being so close to him. It feels warm and right, and not just because the sun is starting to part behind the clouds.

"What do you mean?"

"I think he sent you to me...I mean, I know my family sent me to you, but you are just so much like Nate."

"Ella, I don't want you to be attracted to me because I'm 'like' someone you once loved. I'm my own person."

"Of course you are, but..."

His hands cupped my face and turned it up so that he could look in my eyes. I wanted his kiss again to know for sure if I was right, but the kiss didn't come. Instead, his expression grew sad and then as if recovering from his own feelings, he turned on his practiced, professional demeanor.

"Ella, this is why we can't be together, and if you want I can refer you to another doctor."

"That's the last thing I want."

"It's not what I want either, but how I'm feeling toward you is not in the least bit professional and given what you've said, that's what you need."

"This is what I need."

My kiss took him off guard and his hands remained at his sides initially, but as I held onto his neck and gently let my tongue slide into his mouth, he responded and grabbed onto my waist. His hands slid over my back, reassuring me that he wanted this as much as I did, and then as if determined not to lose a battle between his body and mind, he put his hands on my hips and gently pushed me away.

"What's wrong?"

"It feels like I'm taking advantage of you...of the situation."

"The situation is amazing."

He looked at me as if he didn't know what I was talking about, so I did the absolute wrong thing and told him.

"At first I felt guilty, like I was cheating on Nate by being with you. But now...now that I'm falling for you I realize that he's still looking after me by bringing us together, and it gives him peace along with me."

He looked at me with total bafflement.

"There's just too many coincidences. There's no other explanation."

"Other than what, Ella?"

"I think you are Nate reincarnated."

And that's when he flat out turned me down.

Chapter 32 - Ethan

The doctor in me wanted to stay, but the guy who had his hands all over her just minutes earlier was telling me to get out. It's never a great idea to date a girl who is hung up on someone else, much less a ghost. Not that I believed in ghosts. I just thought she had more issues than any of us had realized...or that I had chosen to ignore.

"Listen, I'm going to try and be patient here," I said running my hands through my hair. "Walk with me," I asked.

She followed behind as I hurried back toward the trail head marker. "You look stressed. Ethan, don't freak."

"I'm not freaking; I'm just...trying to understand you."

"It's simple," Ella told me as if talking to a child. "Nate's ghost used to visit me, but once I started to fall for you, our time together became more infrequent."

"But you still believe in ghosts?"

"No, of course not...not *all* ghosts. But I can see Nate."

I rolled my eyes. "Then why can't I?"

"Because he doesn't need to be here when you're here."

"Ella, don't you see that only means you're starting to recover from the trauma of your accident? It has nothing to do with ghosts. It's about you moving on with your life."

"That's not true," she said in a quiet voice. "How do I get you to believe?"

I shook my head, both in answer to her question and frustration. This was why I should have never crossed that line. I wanted to believe her, if only so I could be with her, but that's not what she needed.

We had come full circle. Our hike ended where it began. We had made our way back to the highway and I was once again only her doctor. It had to be that way. A sudden chill hit me. The sun was dipping low in the sky and darkness would fall soon.

"I'm sorry, Ella. I can't risk falling in love with you only to be a third wheel in this relationship."

"You're not."

I looked at her with doubt, knowing that she not only still loved Nate, but believed that he was with her. Maybe she was right. There were too many strange coincidences to ignore. Regardless, I wanted her for myself.

"Ella, I'm sorry. There are too many reasons why I can't do this."

Tears started to flow down her face and I wanted to take her in my arms, but she was running for her car and had hit the unlock button on her keys. The car chirped in response, the only sound in the quiet of the outdoors other than her choked sobs. She got in and drove off.

Chapter 33 - Nate

The look that Ella wore on her face was one that made my heart drop to my knees. I had seen that look before on men who had been told they had lost their best friend. I could only imagine what it was like for the families back home. The knock on the door by nameless soldiers, dressed immaculately but carrying the news of war. Ella looked as if she had been to battle.

I touched her arm gently and she turned to see me sitting next to her. Probably not the best idea since she was crying and behind the wheel.

"It's okay," I said in a voice that was meant to be both soothing and commanding. "Just pull over for a minute."

She guided the car to the shoulder of the road, nearly three miles from where she had left Ethan. The terrain of this area was slightly more rugged than where we used to hike, but no less beautiful. The sign along the narrow shoulder indicated that parking wasn't permitted, but it was still a safer alternative than to allow Ella to drive while feeling so vulnerable, and what I suspected was an emotion of recklessness.

"Can we walk?" she asked, placing her hand on my cheek.

"There's only half an hour or so of light left. Isn't it better here?" I said trying to reason that we should stay put.

She shook her head, looking desperate to recapture what we used to have together.

"Alright, come on then."

The embankment from the highway down to the woods was steep and it would take the balance and agility of a gazelle to navigate downward to any area that was worthy of a walk. Still, Ella didn't mind and insisted that we go for it. Holding her hand, I helped her down, careful to lead her away from the thorny underbrush and sudden drops in the earth caused by pesky gophers and perhaps snake holes.

Having a ghost as a guide certainly has its advantages and she made it to the flat terrain unharmed and in record time. The minute we were out of sight from the threat of passing cars, I took her in my arms. She buried her head in my chest and we both held on tight.

"I miss you every day, Nate. I can't do this without you. I thought it was getting better, but..."

"Ethan..."

"You know about him."

She said it as a statement, not a question.

"He's a good guy. Give him time."

As if uncomfortable with her own feelings, she changed the subject. "Are you going to leave again?"

"I'll be here...as long as you need me." I took Ella in my arms and smoothed down her hair, letting my hand trail down her back. I moved my hand in small circles, until she audibly exhaled. She used to fall asleep in my arms while I did this and even now, as the air grew colder, I could feel her relax into me. I hated to ruin the moment.

"But Ella...one day you're going to be fine on your own. You have to believe that."

"Not quite yet, Nate. I can't lose you just yet."

Chapter 34 - Ella

All I wanted to do was show Ethan the places that I used to frequent with Nate. I wasn't trying to compare them, but everything I said turned out wrong. And now I've lost him too. It feels a bit like the day of the accident, an overwhelming ache in my stomach.

I just want some lightness back in my life...some way to feel alive. I look up at Nate and smile mischievously. "First one to that tree gets my last granola bar," and I take off before he can respond.

I'm running at full throttle, loving the feel of the wind whipping my hair around. But I can hear Nate's footsteps keeping pace just behind me. It's not like I can outrun a Marine.

"Yeah, try and beat me," he said without even the decency to be out of breath. He was as fit as the day he entered the Marines and a ghost. It was no wonder he caught me so easily.

Nate caught my hand and held it firmly. I would have stumbled on the rough terrain, but as always, he was there to catch me. He pulled me into his arms and pressed his mouth to mine. My heart was beating wildly, both from the exertion of the run and the feel of his kiss.

We separated and I looked up at him. "God, I miss that. I miss it so much," I said, the tears flowing freely now.

"Sshhh, don't...don't cry. You'll always have me in your heart."

"Don't you see, Nate? That's just not enough anymore."

"Maybe it has to be. You keep me here," he said, pressing a hand to his own heart, "...and give Ethan a chance to heal yours."

"That's not going to happen," I said sadly, although I felt guilty for letting my torn emotions show.

Nate raised an eyebrow at me. The look said that he wanted to help, but I knew he wouldn't really want the details. I took his hand and started up a steep incline. "Help me up here?"

"Come on, Ella," he said giving my arm a slight tug. "It's time for you to go home."

"I just can't. If Lily is at home, you won't be there, and as for Ethan..." I let my voice trail off.

"What? Just tell me."

"Why are your visits so infrequent when I spend time with him? It's related, isn't it?"

He nodded sadly. "You need to move on, and I'm here to help you. But sometimes, it doesn't seem like I'm doing that. But when Ethan is with you, there's a light on again."

"I told him...about you."

"Oh Ella." Nate shook his head and then ran his hand through his hair. I had been comparing Ethan's habits to Nate, but in that action I saw Ethan. They wore the same frustrated and sad look.

"Not you too, Nate. I can't take any more pity glances, like I'm damaged and crazy."

The incline was steep, but I was determined to get to the top. I wanted to be up high to see the world from a different vantage point, to get some insight into why I was so messed up and maybe find the answers. I used my hands to brace myself over the rock formations. The climb was hard work, but it served to warm up my body from the dropping temperatures.

"Ella, you have to go home. I can't protect you from threats that are alive -- the cold is enough to harm you, but what about mountain lions, rattlers and the rest? It's practically dark. I can't stay if you don't want me to."

I stopped for a moment and turned to see Nate's beautiful eyes, showing concern and begging me to turn back around, but I needed to think, to make sense of my life once and for all. Was I seeing a ghost or simply holding onto my memories, and if so, was that so wrong? Chasing this shadow was the only thing that had made me feel whole in the wake of so much sorrow, that is until Ethan came along. And now, I felt a myriad of emotions vacillating in my mind, from guilt of betraying Nate's memory to feeling a sense of entitlement that I deserved to be happy.

Nate's image was fading from my vision. It always did when I thought of Ethan. I pulled him back into my mind and saw him once more. He held out his hand to me, begging me to turn around, but I wasn't ready to go home just yet.

I kept going.

Chapter 35 - Ethan

When she drove off, my instinct was to follow her, but I'm the one that said I couldn't have a relationship. If that's true, then why does this feel a bit like a break-up? I drove over Mulholland Highway, following the gentle curves of the road back toward Calabasas and then into Old Town where I planned to grab a beer and clear my head before going home.

The parking lot of the Sage Brush Cantina was full of bikers, their usual Sunday hangout. As I walked through the outdoor patio, someone called my name.

"Hey, it's good to see you," I said to Marc, a friend who I haven't seen since medical school.

"What are you doing here? Join me. My girlfriend is going to be late."

I pulled up a chair, happy to have the company, although Marc immediately launched into questions that I wasn't in the mood to answer.

"So Ethan, how's residency? You dating anyone?"

I thought how ironic it was that the answer to both questions led me to think of Ella.

"Fine and no."

Marc gave me a questioning glance. "That sounds enthusiastic," he said with a sarcastic response.

"There's a girl," I answered simply.

"Ahh, it's always a girl. Let me get the next round and you tell me all about it. I'll dump my dermatologist training and play psychologist."

I laughed. It felt good because if I didn't know better, I'd say that I was totally head over heels for Ella and I just told her I couldn't be with her. When Marc got back with two icy beers and a bowl of pretzels for good measure, he sat and opened his palms to me, a gesture that said I should launch into my story.

I admitted to him that she had gotten under my skin the moment I met her. That even when she was in the hospital wearing an ugly cotton gown that tied in the back and featured the standard pattern of pale blue dots, she still looked beautiful.

"How crazy is that?" I asked, remembering that I thought she looked sexy in a hospital gown.

"That's mildly inappropriate considering you were her doctor."

"You don't have to tell me. That's what I'm saying."

"But, then again, when you're not in your office or a hospital setting, you aren't technically on duty...so..."

"But I was still trying to help her. I only saw her in an outdoor setting because I thought it would help her to open up to me."

"Well, captain...mission accomplished."

I gave him a weary smile. "What do I do? I really like this girl."

"It's not that hard. Resign from her case, date her, and help her out the way any friend or boyfriend would. Isn't that what we all do? Listen? Talk? It's no different from what we're doing now."

"Except I don't have any desire to kiss you. No offense."

"None taken, but I thought you always told me that I had the prettiest eyes." Marc gave me a friendly punch in the shoulder. "You should go after her, you know."

"You think?"

"Definitely."

"I don't even know where she lives," I said, shaking my head at the thought that was brewing. "But...I do have access to her hospital records."

"I won't tell."

"Thanks, buddy."

Marc downed the rest of his beer and I did the same, suddenly in a hurry to leave the bar. "Go get her," he said, before we both exited.

# # #

It took me less than five minutes at my office computer to locate Ella's address and just five more to get back into my car and head toward the quiet Agoura Hills neighborhood where she was living. The records indicated she lived at her sister's house, and I assumed she had probably moved in shortly after the accident.

She had been through a lot in the last few months and as I drove, I started feeling guilty for adding to any stress that she faced due to my wayward thoughts that told me to kiss her one minute and run for the hills the next.

"If only she hadn't insisted on going hiking..." I said aloud as I turned onto the street where she lived. "And if she wasn't so damn pretty, funny, and smelled like flowers! Geez, get a grip."

I took a deep breath as I parked the car next to the curb of a well-manicured lawn and made my way up the path to the front door.

The door opened abruptly, before I even had a chance to knock and I found myself staring at a woman that was slightly older than Ella with the same soulful brown eyes.

"Oh, I thought you were someone else," she spoke curtly, and seemingly disappointed at my arrival. "What can I do for you?"

I held out my hand. "Hi, I'm Ethan. I was hoping to see Ella."

She grabbed my hand and pulled me inside while speaking at once, her tone going from hurried to worried. "She told me she was with you."

"She isn't home?" I said, looking up the stairs for any sign that Ella was hidden above. "She left before me. Where we were...it isn't that far from here."

"What's going on? Did you make plans to meet here?"

My face fell. "No, it's nothing like that. We..."

The hesitation in my voice gave way to her rising panic. "Why are you here? If you went hiking and she left, then I assume you left too. Why didn't you just go home, do whatever you have planned for the evening? What's going on between you two?"

"We sort of had an argument."

"How can you have an argument? You're her therapist."

I looked at the floor, feeling duly chastised. I had to tell her. I could lose my license, but I owed her. I also wanted to say it out loud. I had fallen in love with Ella and I would do anything to help her. And so I came in and we sat down, and I told her everything. By the time I was finished, it was obvious to both of us that Ella was clearly in trouble.

"Do you think she went back to the mountain?" Lily asked.

"I know she finds comfort there," I answered carefully, not wanting to disclose the information I knew about her visions, or whatever she would call them, of Nate.

"You mean, she finds Nate there."

I looked at Lily directly. "Do you believe her?"

Lily looked at the ceiling and shook her head, searching for an answer. "I know that they had a connection that not many people find and it makes sense that she isn't willing to let that connection die along with him. But, she also seemed genuinely happy about meeting you. She didn't tell me everything, obviously..." she paused, "but she did have a certain girlish giddiness when talking about you. It makes sense now and I wouldn't deny the two of you being together."

"I didn't intend for this to happen."

"I know. We never know who we're going to fall in love with."

I looked at her with shock. I hadn't realized it until she verbalized those words. I had fallen in love with a patient.

"It's okay, Ethan," Lily said and touched my sleeve. "In my mind, the situation would only be wrong if you didn't love her. Let's get you back together and this will never go beyond these walls."

I stood up and grabbed my coat from the couch. "You call search and rescue. I'm going back. Do you have some blankets I can take?"

She nodded and went to an antique chest to pull out a few, then crossed to the kitchen to retrieve a backpack that she placed some bottles of water, dried fruit, nuts, and beef jerky.

She handed me the makeshift emergency supply kit and our eyes met.

"Temperatures are supposed to drop to freezing later tonight."

I nodded. "I've got extra clothes in the car; I have to go."

"You could let the professionals do this. You don't have to."

"For my heart and my very soul...I'm going to find her."

Chapter 36 - Nate

I didn't survive Afghanistan, where I witnessed countless men who had lost their lives, only to come home and lose Ella. But I did...in an accident. We were lucky enough to be given a second chance with each other, the opportunity to see and feel each other. It's both miraculous and crazy. The car accident was just that...an accident, unavoidable and unforeseen. But losing her now would be pure recklessness and I had to bring her back, even if it meant losing her again to someone else.

Yet the idea of her finding love again would be preferable to having her life taken before its rightful time. As God is my witness, I'm going to find her

Acknowledgments

Without Jessica Molina Ramirez my books would not see the light of day -- or if they did, they'd certainly have more typos and editing errors. Short Side of Tall Editing has become my saving grace as have you with your clever marketing, sunny disposition, and I'm so pleased to say, your friendship.

Ginelle Blanch and Gabrielle Warner -- thank you for pre-reading my books and keeping me on my toes so that they're ready for other eyes as well.

Lisa Markson -- thank you for being so organized and taking care of the details that helped to spread the word about "Believe."

My street team -- thank you for 'believing' in me.

Bob Houston for always being a formatter extraordinaire.

"Believe" cover design was created by phatpuppyart with photography by Teresa Yeh and typography by Catie Crehan.

Stay in touch with Mia Fox

Learn about upcoming books including the exciting conclusion to the Chasing Shadows Series, known as "Trust."
www.miafox.net
www.facebook.com/MiaFoxBooks
www.twitter.com/MiaFoxBooks
www.pinterest.com/MiaFoxBooks
www.instagram.com/MiaFoxBooks

Other books by Mia Fox

The Romani Realms Series
Released (book 1)
Resurrected (book 2)
Returned (book 3) -- coming Fall 2014

The Hollywood Hottie Series
Alert the Media (book 1)
Keeping Up (book 2) -- coming Winter 2014

The Surprise Passion Series (Mia Fox writing as Lola Bond)
Ready for the Yeti (book 1)
Going Steady with the Yeti (book 2)
Ethel and the Merman (book 3) -- coming Spring 2014

Evatopia Press

For more information about Evatopia Press visit http://www.evatopia.com/

Learn more about other Evatopia Press authors...

Lizzy Ford –
http://www.guerillawordfare.com/

Cambria Hebert –
http://cambriahebert.com/

Cindy Mezni –
http://www.cindymezni.com/

Melissa Pearl –
http://melissapearlauthor.com